Sue Welford

Sue Welford was born in Brighton, Sussex. She has two children and lives in Kent with her family and two Jack Russell terriers. *Catch the Moon* was her first published book (it originally appeared in 1989), followed by *Secrets* in 1990. Since then, Sue has had several books published including *The Ghost in the Mirror*, which was shortlisted for the Whitbread Award, and *The Night After Tomorrow*, winner of the Angus Book Award.

Also in the **Contents** series

Also by Sue Welford

Contents

Sue Welford

The Shadow of August

Mammoth

First published in Great Britain 1995
by Oxford University Press
Published 1997 by Mammoth
an imprint of Reed International Books Ltd
Michelin House, 81 Fulham Road, London SW3 6RB
and Auckland and Melbourne

Copyright © Sue Welford 1995

The moral rights of the author and cover illustrator have been asserted

ISBN 0 7497 2746 2

10 9 8 7 6 5 4 3 2 1

A CIP catalogue record for this title
is available from the Britsih Library

Printed in Great Britain
by Cox & Wyman Ltd, Reading, Berkshire

S u e   W e l f o r d

The Shadow of August

Mattie

1

The hand Mattie held in hers was almost transparent. Even the fingernails seemed to weigh it down. It moved feebly in Mattie's. Mattie stared at her mother's pale, yellowish face. I should feel something, she thought. I should be crying. But all she could feel was a numbness in face of the knowledge that the armies of her mother's cancer had almost won their battle for her life.

Mattie stroked her mother's clammy forehead. Several long strands of hair came away beneath her fingers. She wiped them off on the knee of her jeans so no one would see. Her mother's pain-filled eyes opened. Mattie's heart drummed. She felt guilty. Could Mum see that all she really wanted to do was run away and scream? She glanced up. There were two misty figures within the shadow of the moving curtain by the open window. One, the smaller of the two, the woman, began to move towards Mattie. Her arms were outstretched as if to comfort her. Mattie tore her eyes away.

'Mattie?' Mary's voice was harsh and dry. Her eyes wandered as if she strove to see a far distant speck on the horizon.

Mattie screwed her face into some kind of a smile. She ran her thumb over the bird bones of her mother's hand.

'Yes, Mum. I'm here. Everything's OK.'

Liar, she thought. Everything's terrible. She glanced up again but the figures had gone.

'Mattie . . .' Mary said again. The eyes focused and moved slowly round Mattie's face. 'I want to tell you something.'

A nurse bustled in. Her rubber soles squeaked on the vinyl floor. She carried a kidney-shaped dish. The end of a syringe stuck out beneath a white cloth. She put her hand on Mattie's shoulder.

'Why don't you go and get a cup of tea, Mattie?'

Mattie was suddenly aware of someone rattling past with a trolley. It was laden with a shiny tea-urn, polystyrene cups, Kit-Kats and Mars bars and packets of crisps. It seemed absurdly cheerful in this place of sadness. How could people eat Mars bars and crisps when so many people were dying and there was nothing anyone could do to stop them?

Behind came Katherine, her mother's friend. The roses she held were the colour of blood. Mattie sighed with relief. If she wasn't careful she'd lose control. Run out of the hospice and never come back. It was miracle cures that were needed, not cups of tea and Kit-Kats.

She got up slowly and pushed back the chair. 'I'll be back in a minute, Mum,' she said gently. 'Katherine's here to see you. OK?'

'How is she?' Katherine's eyes were upon the pallid face, the hand clutching nervously at the sheet's edge.

Mattie smiled down at her mother. Her eyes brimmed and she seemed to be looking at her from the bottom of a pool of water. Her mother's blue-veined eyelids had closed. Whatever it was she had wanted to tell her daughter would have to wait.

Mattie swallowed. 'She's a bit better today, aren't you, Mum?'

Katherine's glance met Mattie's as she shrugged hopelessly. There was no pulling the wool over Katherine's eyes. She could see as well as anyone that Mary was ten times worse. Katherine squeezed her arm. 'Go and get that tea, Mattie, you look as if you need it.'

Mattie bent and kissed Mary's sunken cheek. 'Won't be long, Mum.'

Mary's lids fluttered open. Her arm rose as if to hold on to her. Mattie stayed where she was but the arm fell back and her mother closed her eyes against the pain.

***

'Will you be all right here on your own, Mattie?' Katherine dried the twentieth cup and put it away in the cupboard. The remains of Mattie's attempt at a Victoria sponge lay like a ruined castle on a plate by the microwave.

'I'll be fine.' Mattie was used to looking after herself. Her mother had had spells in hospital before and once she was old enough, Mattie had stayed at the flat on her own. Anyway, Mary had always worked outside the home. Right from the age of seven or eight Mattie had been a latchkey kid. But she had always been bright—mature for her age—and she'd managed all right then.

Mattie tipped the dirty washing-up water down the sink and squeezed out the cloth. She felt her eyes fill. She swallowed quickly. The funeral had been a nightmare. Mum's colleagues from work sniffing into lipstick-stained tissues. Her boss, his face flushed from too much sherry, giving Mattie a hug so close she could smell yesterday's garlic on his breath. The priest. Saying all that stuff about Mary when he had never even known her. That awful hat the woman from the bookshop wore. Mum would have cracked up if she'd seen it. Mattie didn't know why she'd come to the funeral anyway. Mary was a good customer but hardly the woman's bosom pal. Strangely, though, it seemed they had been closer than Mattie knew.

'She used to talk to me a lot,' the woman had said tearfully. 'We had so much in common.'

'Did you?' Mattie had been surprised. She never really thought Mary had much in common with anybody.

'Yes,' the woman had sniffed. 'We came from the same kind of background, you see. I shall really miss our little chats. They did us both good. Mary told me things about herself that I don't think anyone else ever knew.' The woman had gone off, dabbing her eyes with a handkerchief, with Mattie promising to visit her sometime. She had

5

watched the woman go, head bowed, that ridiculous hat skew-whiff where she had dislodged it hugging Mattie.

Katherine put an arm round Mattie's shoulders. 'You know you can come and live with us. I promised your mum . . .'

Mattie smiled. 'Thanks, Katherine. But I'd rather stay here.'

Another lie, Mattie thought. All she really wanted to do was go off somewhere . . . Sri Lanka . . . Australia . . . some exotic palm-fringed shore . . . the moon? Anywhere . . . She had often thought she'd take off somewhere. Especially after some row or other with her mother over some petty thing had left her upset and puzzled. Mattie had always known her mother was neurotic . . . obsessed by some things that others took for granted. That's why she'd had those spells in hospital.

'She just needs to retreat from the world for a while,' the doctor had told Mattie.

'From me?' Mattie had said the first time it happened.

'No.' The doctor had held both her hands. 'Not you, Mattie. Just the pressures of being a lone parent in a tough old world. We can arrange for you to go into care if you like.'

But Katherine had always taken her in until she was old enough to stay by herself. After all, what were best friends for?

Some of their rows had been over such ridiculous things they had been hard to forget. Things like the time Mattie had wanted to go away on a school trip. An adventure centre in Cornwall. Mary had gone barmy. Things happened to children at adventure centres. They fell out of canoes, over cliffs, off horses. Mattie had cried and pleaded but it had been no good. Mary refused to let her go. Then there was that time Mattie had said she'd like to be a police officer when she grew up. Mary had stormed at her for days. It was no job for a woman . . . you might get stabbed, beaten, meet all sorts of criminals . . . psychopaths . . . serial killers.

In the end, Mattie had promised she would never think about becoming a policewoman again.

Mattie sighed. She leaned her palms on the sink and gazed out of the window. She had loved her mother but life with Mary hadn't been easy.

Mattie turned and gazed round the room. She'd lived in this flat for over half of her life. The way the sun fell on its windows, the angles of its walls, the sound the door handles made, were as familiar to her as her own reflection. She turned back to the window. A flock of pigeons rose from the pavement below as a red Mini screeched to a halt in front of the steps. The door swung open. A boy with long legs and a shock of pale hair tied back in a pony-tail at the nape of his neck unfolded from the driver's seat on to

up to the front door three steps at a time.

'Bram's here,' said Mattie. She felt guilty at the strange, sudden feeling of release. There would be no more interrogations about her relationship with Bram. No more questions about what they *did* together. Mattie knew that if it hadn't been for the fact that Bram was Katherine's son, Mary would never have let her go out with him. Mattie bit her lip. She *had* to stop feeling guilty . . .

Katherine took off Mary's apron and hung it on the peg behind the door. 'He's really upset he couldn't get here in time for the funeral.'

'I know,' said Mattie. 'He phoned earlier.'

The doorbell screeched. Katherine picked up her handbag and hat from the sofa. She gave Mattie a hug. 'I'll leave you two alone. Now don't forget . . . Any time you want to come and stay.' Tears escaped and ran down her cheeks. 'Poor Mary. I'm so sorry, Mattie.'

The doorbell screamed again and Bram yelled through the letter box. 'Mattie . . . Mum? You in there?'

Mattie smelt Katherine's perfume as she hugged her. It gave her an odd feeling of comfort. Katherine had worn the same scent for years and whenever Mattie smelt it, it

7

reminded her of the good times she'd had with the family when she was a kid. 'Thanks,' she said, sniffing. 'I'll remember.'

Katherine went to open the door.

Bram's intense blue eyes were wide with concern. 'Mum! Is Mattie all right?'

'Yes,' Katherine said. 'But I wish she'd cry.'

Night drew itself in over the city.

'Shall I pull the curtains?'

They were sitting on the sofa. The cat, Sinbad, was curled up on Mattie's lap. He had roamed the flat looking for Mary then decided Mattie would do instead.

Mattie lifted her head from Bram's shoulder. 'No. I like to see the lights.'

They'd been sitting like that for hours. Talking.

'You're going to stay on at college?' Bram had asked.

'Yes.' Mattie had another year before her course was finished. 'I promised Mum.'

Mary had been very keen on Mattie's college course. 'I never had the chance,' she'd said. 'School, a couple of O levels and then stuck in an office for the rest of my life.'

'Didn't you even have time off when I was a baby?' Mattie had asked.

Mary had looked at her sideways. 'A few months,' she'd said cautiously. 'But I had to earn the money to keep us.'

'Yes.' Mattie couldn't remember the childminder. There had been no mention of Mattie's dad. Not until she had asked her mum one day when she was seven years old. 'I'll tell you when you're older,' Mary had said, strangely not yelling at her for asking too many questions.

And when Mattie was older:

'It was just a holiday affair,' Mary explained. 'I didn't want to marry him. I didn't even tell him.' She had hugged Mattie close. 'I wanted you all to myself.'

There had been no men since then . . . no boyfriends

around the place like other girls without dads. Just Mary. And Mattie.

Mary had told Mattie once about her own loveless childhood. Her cold, indifferent mother, her strict father who believed that if you spared the rod, you spoiled the child.

'He put me off men for life,' she'd said bitterly. 'And when I grew up, all I wanted was a baby I could love. And you were it.'

'Lucky you met that bloke on holiday then,' Mattie had said lightly. She knew Mary's unhappy childhood was the ~~of her b~~reakdowns although she had been secretly

Mattie stirred in Bram's arms. 'I've got to see the solicitor tomorrow.'

'About your mum's will?'

Mattie shrugged. 'I suppose so.'

'Do you want me to come with you?'

She looked up into his eyes. 'If you want but I'll be OK on my own.'

Bram kissed the top of her head and rose to turn on the TV. There was a comedy show . . . some twit dressed up like a Viking. Bram laughed suddenly then clapped his hand over his mouth. 'God . . . sorry!'

'Don't be daft.'

Life must go on, everyone had said. Everyone's but Mary's, that was.

Mattie rose. 'I'm starving . . .' She even felt guilty about being hungry, as if the grief should have taken away her appetite. 'I've only had a bit of disaster cake since breakfast. Do you fancy something to eat?'

'I'll go down and get a Chinese if you like?'

'Great.'

Bram fumbled in his jeans pocket.

'I've got some money.' She went to the sideboard drawer and took out a tenner. Mum had always kept money in the house. 'Here . . . get it with this.'

The comedy show on TV had finished and had changed to a nature programme. The titles were rolling. They were accompanied by a surge of classical music and film of sunlight streaming, shadows dancing on the dappled grass beneath.

Mattie caught sight of the screen as she turned to give Bram the money. Then she drew in her breath. By the window she saw the man. He was bending over doing something with his hands. She heard bird-song then realized it came from the television. The man looked back at her and smiled. Then suddenly, he was gone. Mattie felt a surge of panic, a feeling of loss so great that she burst into tears.

Bram was staring at her. 'Mattie . . .!'

'And you've always seen them?' Bram had waited patiently, holding her in the circle of his arms until the storm passed. Until at last she was able to tell him what, finally, had opened the floodgates. He held her at arm's length and was staring at her, his eyes frowning with disbelief.

Mattie sniffed and blew her nose. The tears, when they came, had been hot and uncontrollable and had lasted all the way through the nature programme and well into the news.

She nodded. 'Yes. Ever since I can remember.'

'Just here . . . in this flat?'

'No, wherever we lived. When I was little we moved loads of times. Mum dragged me all over the place until she finally settled here. They always came with us.'

'Us? Could Mary see them too?'

Mattie shook her head. 'No . . . only me.'

'How do you know?'

'I asked her once who the people were standing by the

river when we were out for a picnic. She just laughed and said I was seeing things so I never mentioned it again. And I said something about them to someone at school once but they thought I was barmy.'

Bram was looking at her as if she was mad as well. 'Mat... you're sure . . .? I mean, most kids have imaginary frie... ...face, he broke off.

...ight have known

'...
I've ever ...

Mattie tuck... ear. 'Do you thi... ...deep brown, red-rimmed eyes flash...

Bram shook his head quickly. 'No . . . of course not. I'm sorry, Mattie.'

'Honestly, Bram. I do see them. A man and a woman.' OK, so he didn't believe her but she still felt relieved. As if she had at last shed a burden she'd been carrying round all her life. She realized suddenly just how much she had wanted to tell him. How long she had been waiting for the right moment to come.

'What are they, then?' Perhaps he was beginning to think it was true after all? 'Ghosts?'

'I just don't know.'

'Don't they scare you?'

Bram rubbed his hand round his jaw. He'd been travelling home from France with his dad since early that morning and badly needed a shave.

She shook her head. 'No . . . because they've always been there. It's as if they're part *of* me, if you know what I mean.

And besides, they're always smiling. They're always looking at me and smiling.'

'How often do you see them?'

'Sometimes not for ages . . . months . . . Once I went a
year and didn't see them. I felt sad because I thought they'd
gone for ever. Then suddenly I'll look up and they'll be
there. Sometimes I'll see them twice in one day . . . like
today.'

'When you're upset, or tired?'

She bit her lip. It was no good, he still didn't really
believe her. He thought she was having hallucinations. That
the two people who seemed to have been with her all her
life were just figments of her imagination. Yet, to Mattie,
they were as real as Bram was. 'I don't know . . . maybe,'
she said. 'What are you trying to say, Bram?'

'I'm just trying to find a rational explanation.'

'There isn't one, Bram. Don't you think I've tried and
tried? I've read books on the paranormal . . . psychology
books . . . everything, to try and find out if seeing people's
the first sign of losing your marbles.'

'And?'

'There only seem to be two explanations. Either I'm
psychic or I'm mad.'

Bram smiled and took both her hands in his. 'You're not
mad, Mattie. In fact, you're probably the most sane person
I've ever met, that's why I love you.'

Mattie shrugged. 'So that means I'm psychic, OK?'

Bram was still frowning. 'Have you ever seen anything
else . . . well, paranormal?'

She shook her head. 'No, nothing. I don't really even
believe in that kind of stuff.' She raised her eyebrows. 'I
mean I'd *like* to believe it but until I actually see something
that convinces me . . .'

'Do they talk to you?'

'No.' Mattie was getting agitated. Why was he giving her
the third degree? Why couldn't he just accept what she
said? 'Not really.'

'Maybe you should tell someone . . . you know, your doctor. She's been a good friend to you, hasn't she?'

'Bram, I'm not ill.' She ran her thumb over the back of Bram's hand. Then she looked up at him, eyes bright. It would be like one of her worst nightmares come true. 'Anyway, she'll refer me to a psychiatrist, I know she will. Family history and all that . . .'

'Mattie, you're not a bit like your mum, everybody knows that.'

Mattie drew a deep breath. She suddenly felt tired. So tired she could sleep for a week.

'I know,' she said. 'But I'm still too scared to tell anybody. I don't want them sending me off to some psychiatric place . . . not like Mum.'

'Mattie, they won't.'

'Bram, you must promise me you won't tell anyone.'

If she couldn't trust him then she couldn't trust anyone.

Bram grinned and put his arm round her. She rested her head beneath his chin. 'Your secret's safe with me, Mattie. And they didn't *put* your mum away . . . she volunteered.' He kissed the top of her head then held her away from him. 'But you *should* try to find out who, or what, they are, you know. It's obviously bugging you.'

'But how?' she said bleakly.

Bram shrugged 'I don't know, Mattie.'

She extricated herself from his arms. 'I'm tired, Bram, let's talk about it tomorrow, huh?'

'What about that Chinese?'

But she wasn't hungry any more.

'Shall I stay?' he asked when she told him she didn't fancy anything to eat after all.

Bram had only been staying overnight since her mother went to the hospice. Mattie had felt so guilty at first. Having a boy in her bed when her mum had warned her against them so many times.

But tonight, although she needed him more than ever, she wanted to be alone. Just her and the cat and her ghosts who weren't ghosts at all. She didn't want to think about all the empty evenings that stretched ahead. Not now.

'I'm sorry,' she said again. She kissed him.

Bram kissed her back. 'It's OK, I understand. I'll be round first thing.'

She watched as he drove away. The red tail-lights of the Mini disappeared along the deserted street. In the distance, the hum of the traffic was like a bee-swarm.

Mattie drew the curtains.

On the piano was a picture of her mother. Katherine had taken it one day when they'd all gone to the sea. Mattie and Mary. Katherine and Bram. His sister, Jo, their dad, James. Mattie remembered James had held her hand as they walked along the sea wall. She felt kind of special, having this big man hold her small hand in his. Nothing like that had ever happened to her before.

She picked up the photo and gazed at it. Mary had always been shy of having her photograph taken. There were none of her as a young woman . . . none even of Mattie until she had started school. It was hard to remember Mary's fair hair, the blue eyes, the thin mouth. All Mattie could see was the eyes bright with pain, the skin shiny and sunken, the hair that came out in handfuls. They had laughed at first, saying it would grow back better, thicker than before, as if going bald at forty-two was a joke. But it didn't grow back and now it never would.

Mattie lay in bed, eyes wide against the dark. It was past midnight. The street lights had dimmed to an orange glow. Patterns danced on the wall as the light from the neon sign outside the Chinese Take-Away flashed on and off. The cat, curled by her feet, ignored the two shadowy figures standing in front of the window. Their faces were grey, like a reflection in a misted mirror. But Mattie knew they smiled. They simply always did.

The figures glided towards her then loomed over the bed. Their faces were huge, as they always were when they came close.

14

'Peek-a-boo.' The man put his hands over his face then took them away. 'Peek-a-boo.' His soft voice echoed round the room like the whisper of passing breezes.

Mattie stared at them; the dark hair and dark shadowed eyes. The rest was grey and misty like looking through a fog. She seemed to hear a whispered name.

But, strangely, it wasn't hers.

2

The solicitor's office was in a grey stone building. A shiny brass plaque outside the door said the firm was on the fifth floor.

Bram held Mattie's hand as they waited for the lift.

'Have you met this guy before?'

'It's a woman. And no, I didn't even know Mum *had* a solicitor until someone rang up. Mum had asked the hospice to tell them when she . . .' Mattie swallowed. She couldn't quite say it yet. Somehow, actually saying the word 'died' might prevent all possibility of it not being true. Of it being just some ghastly nightmare from which she couldn't wake.

Bram squeezed her hand.

A secretary sat frowning at a word processor. She looked up and smiled as they went in.

'Mattie Browne,' said Mattie.

'Oh, yes. Mrs Hodson's just on the phone. She won't keep you a minute.'

'Thanks.' Mattie sat down. The office was dreary. Brown paint, yellow wallpaper. Someone had attempted to cheer the place up by hanging up a picture of a field of poppies and sunflowers. Mattie was reminded of fried eggs and tomato sauce. A drooping plant in the corner looked as if it was dying of thirst.

'Do you want me to come in with you?' Bram whispered in her ear.

'No, it's OK, thanks. I don't suppose I'll be more than a few minutes.'

Mattie couldn't think her mother's affairs would take long to sort out. The flat . . . a few savings . . . not a lot to show for a short life of hard work and worry. Unless you counted Mattie, of course. Mary had always said Mattie was her greatest achievement.

Someone buzzed and the secretary looked up. 'You can go in now.'

'Thanks.'

Mrs Hodson seemed dwarfed by her enormous desk. She rose and held out her neatly manicured hand as Mattie went in. 'Mattie, I'm so sorry about your mother.'

'Thanks,' Mattie said flatly.

'Please, sit down. Would you like some coffee?'

'No, thanks.'

Please, Mattie thought, just get on with it. She crossed and uncrossed her feet nervously. Her fingers twisted themselves together in her lap.

The solicitor opened a file in front of her. Then she gazed at Mattie from behind gold-rimmed spectacles. 'Mattie, everything of your mother's goes to you, of course.'

'Yes.' Mattie fiddled with the tear in the knee of her jeans. There would be no one to nag her to mend it now. No one to tell her to wear something decent instead of old jeans and a leather jacket she'd got from the Oxfam shop.

'The mortgage on the flat is paid off at your mother's death. And she's managed to save quite a good sum of money. She was very anxious about your future.'

'Yes.' Mattie felt like an answering machine.

'. . . and then, of course, there's the house in Cornwall.'

Mattie took a deep breath. 'Sorry?'

'The house in Cornwall. Your mother's house in Porthland.'

Something cold passed across Mattie's flesh. What on earth was the woman talking about?

She must have gone pale. 'Mattie . . .? Are you all right?'

Mattie gulped. 'Yes, sure. Er . . . what house in Cornwall?'

The woman glanced at her shrewdly. 'You didn't know about it,' she said flatly.

Mattie shook her head. 'No.'

17

The solicitor sighed and shook her head. 'Mary said she was going to tell you.'

A scene flashed. Mum . . . saying she had something to tell her. When Mattie went back to find out what it had been Mum had been asleep.

'She was too sick . . .' Mattie began.

'Yes, of course,' the woman murmured. She thumbed through a sheaf of papers. 'Well, Mattie,' she said brightly. 'It's the house where Mary was brought up. Her mother died six years ago and left it to her.'

Mattie frowned. 'No,' she said quickly. 'Both my grandparents died years ago . . . before I was born.'

Mrs Hodson smiled professionally. 'No, Mattie, your *maternal* grandparents.'

'Yes. That's who I'm on about.' Mattie was getting impatient. Didn't the stupid woman know there weren't any other sort? Everything was skew-whiff. Surely solicitors should get their facts right? 'Mum's parents . . . they died years ago.'

Mrs Hodson took off her glasses and leaned forward. She spoke to Mattie as if she was a child. 'Mattie, I think I'd better explain more clearly.'

Mattie came out looking dazed. Bram tossed the old Sunday supplement back on to the table and jumped up.

'Mattie, you OK?'

She swung her bag up on her shoulder. 'Yes. Let's get out of here.'

Over a Coke she told him the details.

'. . . and she died only six years ago. I don't understand why Mum lied to me.'

'Did you know she didn't get on with them?'

Mattie nodded gloomily. 'Yes. She told me she'd had a big row with them when she was twenty-five. She never spoke to either of them again.'

'What was it about?'

18

Mattie shook her head. 'No idea. She'd never tell me. She said it was all in the past and didn't matter any more.'

'They must have been in contact, though . . . for her mother to leave her the house.'

'No.' Mattie noisily sucked the last of her drink. 'The solicitor put one of those notices in the paper . . . you know . . . if anyone knows the whereabouts blah, blah, blah.'

'And Mary saw it?'

Mattie shrugged. 'She must have done. She was a great one for reading the papers, my mum. She scoured them from back to front every day. She loved those personal columns . . .' She looked at Bram and continued. 'You know . . . Bubblehead please come home—Fatface . . . That kind of stuff. I used to tease her about it.'

'Maybe she was hoping someone would put one in for her?'

Mattie hunched her shoulders and stared out of the window. 'Who knows?' she said bleakly. She was beginning to think there were lots of things about her mother she didn't know. It suddenly seemed as if she had been living with a stranger all her life.

'So tell me about the house,' Bram said. He couldn't hide his excitement.

'There's not much to tell really. It's quite big, apparently. Victorian. It's by the sea.'

'Where?'

'In Cornwall. A place called Porthland.'

'What are you going to do with it, Mattie?'

Mattie shrugged. She felt an odd sense of power . . . the owner of two places. A flat and a house by the sea. Her inheritance. Maybe she should sell them and take that trip round the world she'd promised herself. But why had Mum never told her about it? Why wait until it was too late. And why had she lied about her parents? Mattie's brain was a labyrinth of questions.

'I can't do anything,' she said. 'Someone lives in it. They've been paying Mum rent for six years. They're

19

apparently on a ten year agreement so I couldn't go and live in it even if I wanted to.' She fiddled with the soggy straw then looked at Bram, her eyes swimming in unshed tears. 'She's saved all the rent money in a special account for me.'

Bram took her hand. 'You should be pleased.'

Mattie looked down. 'I am . . . but if she—' She rubbed her free hand across her eyes.

'What?' His fingers strayed across her knuckle bones.

Mattie's head jerked up. 'Maybe we could have used the money to get better treatment for her?'

'No, Mattie,' he said gently. 'I don't think any amount of money would have made any difference.'

Mattie sighed. She relaxed her clenched fists. It was pointless getting uptight about something over which you had no control. 'I suppose not.'

'And she would have hated you spending it on her.'

'Yes.' She suddenly remembered something else. 'And you know what, Bram? Her name wasn't Browne at all . . . it was Hughes.'

Bram looked confused. 'I don't understand, Mattie.'

'She changed her name. She must have done it when she left home.'

'What on earth for?'

Mattie shook her head and looked more miserable than ever. 'Haven't got a clue. I suppose she just wanted to escape and start a new life. Maybe she was scared they'd try to trace her.'

'They must have had a terrible row. Just to run away like that, change your name and never go back.'

'Yes,' said Mattie. 'I've often wondered what about.'

'Didn't she tell you *anything* about her parents?'

Mattie told him what she knew. 'I think she must have really hated them,' she said gloomily.

Bram still held her hand across the table. His eyes were bright with sympathy. 'Hey, I know,' he said suddenly. His face cleared. It wasn't in Bram's nature to be dejected for long. 'Let's go down to Porthland and see it.'

'What? The house?'

'Yes. Look, you're off college for the summer and Dad'll give me time off. It'll be great. We could take the camping gear . . . what do you say?'

Bram was like that. Always on the move . . . doing things on the spur of the moment.

Mattie grinned for the first time that day. 'I don't know.'

'Come on, Mattie. I know it's not exactly Sri Lanka but we'll get there too one day. Right now, you need to get away from all this. Your neighbour will look after Sinbad. It'll be excellent, Mattie.'

She couldn't help being infected with his enthusiasm. Besides, he was right. She *did* need to get away.

'Maybe we'll find out why your mum fell out with her parents,' Bram went on. 'And why she told you they'd died when they hadn't. Someone down there might remember what went on. You must *want* to know?'

Mattie laughed. 'Bram, you're getting carried away.'

'Oh, come on, Mattie!'

His eyes sparkled with merriment.

Mattie was allowing herself to be persuaded. He was right. She *did* want to know. She could still hardly take everything in.

'Bram, there's lots of things I've got to do.' She was making token excuses.

He sat back looking disappointed. 'Like what?'

She screwed up the straw and rammed it into the empty glass. 'Go through Mum's stuff for one thing.'

'You've got all the time in the world for that, Mattie. It'll still be there when we get back.'

'There's the bank account and things to sort out,' she said weakly. She half smiled and looked at him from under her lashes. He was grinning like mad as she knew he would be.

'Mattie, do you think it's a great idea to go to Cornwall or not?'

She grinned wider. 'Yes.'

* * *

'Mattie, that's wonderful.' Katherine hugged her close. 'A house . . . how wonderful.'

'Mum never mentioned it to you, did she?' Mattie asked.

Katherine shook her head. 'Not a word. Where did you say it was?'

'Porthland,' Mattie told her.

'Um.' Katherine frowned. 'That rings a bell.'

'What kind of a bell?' James said, looking up from the TV.

'I don't know. Something happened there. It was in all the papers, I'm sure . . .' she shrugged. 'Ages ago, when Bram was a baby.'

'Oh, *that* long ago,' joked Mattie. Bram was a year older than she was. 'No wonder you can't remember.'

3

Porthland was a small seaside town on the south coast of Cornwall. Before holidaymakers discovered it in the reign of Queen Victoria it had been hardly more than a fishing village. The white cottages that hemmed the small harbour seemed stuck in a timewarp. As did the quayside cobblestones chock-a-block with nets and lobster pots . . . the smell of fish in the air.

The narrow streets were crammed with summer visitors and the campsite was full.

'Now what are we going to do?' Mattie was exhausted from the journey and too many sleepless nights. They'd only been half-way down the M4 when she began to wish they hadn't come. She didn't even know if she *wanted* to see the house. Mary had never been happy there or she would never have left like that. It might be best just to pretend it didn't exist.

Bram slammed the car door and sat looking thoughtful. 'The owner said there's a farmer near here who lets people camp on his land.' He started the engine. 'Let's try him.'

Mattie sighed. 'OK.'

They drove along winding, narrow lanes, green and lace-edged with creamy wild parsley. Then up a steep hill to where a sign said 'Trethowan Farm'.

They drove into the yard. A black and white collie barked furiously from its chain. A motley assortment of hens scratched their living beneath an overhanging straw stack. Bram got out of the car and had a word with the farmer, loading bales of hay into the barn. He came back with a grin on his face.

'Two quid a night,' he said. 'And we can stay as long as we like. There's water and loos. Fancy it, Mattie?'

23

Mattie smiled. She didn't really care where she slept as long as it was warm and dry. 'Great.'

There were only two other tents pitched in the field set high above the farmyard overlooking the sea. Mattie got out and took a deep breath of sea air. It seemed to give her new energy.

She ran to the top of the hill. The edge of the cliff was fenced off. She leaned her elbows on the top and gazed at the view. Porthland was spread out below. The sea looked dotted with a thousand mirrors. The fishing fleet was chugging its way back to the tiny harbour. A flock of seagulls flapped squawking in its wake. There was a small café at the end of the breakwater, its orange sun-umbrellas like flowers against the blue of the sky. It all seemed vaguely familiar. Like a photograph or a painting of a place you look at so many times it seems you might once have been there. She turned to call Bram.

He stopped unloading the car and came and put his arms round her. 'Fantastic,' was all he said.

She leaned against him. 'I know it's crazy but I've got a really strange feeling I've been here before.'

'*Déjà vu*?'

'Yes . . . kind of.'

'Maybe you *have* been here with your mum after all?'

Mattie shook her head. 'I don't know.' She turned to look at him. The wind blew a stray lock of his hair across his eyes. She brushed it back for him and tucked it behind his ear. 'You remember that time we went to the beach with your mum and dad and Jo? The day your mum and Mary had a row because your mum took a photo of her.'

Bram grinned. 'Yep . . . *and* I remember you fell into a rock pool with all your clothes on.'

'You would remember that.' Mattie smiled. 'Well, that was the first time I'd ever been to the seaside . . . don't you remember Mum telling Katherine?'

Bram stuck out his bottom lip and shook his head. 'No, can't say I do.'

24

'Well, I do. I remember Mum telling Katherine she'd never taken me to the beach. So she couldn't have brought me here, could she?'

Bram took her hand and led her back to the car. 'Mattie, I hate to say this, but it seems as if a lot of things your mum told you weren't true.'

Mattie lowered her gaze. 'Yes, I know.' It was all so crazy. What possible reason could her mother have had for lying to her? She plonked herself down on the grass and leaned back against the wheel arch with a sigh.

'Lots of these seaside places are alike . . . it could have been somewhere else,' said Bram, crouching down beside her.

But Mattie was positive. 'No, I recognize the harbour . . . that little café at the end of the breakwater. I know I do. I'm not barmy, Bram.'

'I know,' he said soothingly. 'I'm sorry.' He pulled at her hand. 'Come on, let's put the tent up then we can go and explore. You've got the address of the house . . . your house?'

Mattie patted the back pocket of her jeans. 'Yes.' Then she went on, '*My* house.' She pulled a face. 'It sounds very posh.'

Bram gave her a hug. 'You know I always wanted to go out with a rich woman.'

She snorted air through her nostrils. She'd never wanted to be rich. Only free to do what she liked. Well . . . now she could please herself although, somehow, that longed-for freedom didn't seem quite so desirable now that she'd got it.

It was early evening, the sun low in the sky, before the tent was up and their things unpacked. They called in at the farmhouse on their way down to the town.

'Don't tell them why we're here,' Mattie said as Bram knocked on the door.

Bram glanced at her. 'OK.'

The farmer's wife came to the door. She had a blonde, chubby child on her hip.

'I wondered if you wanted any money?' said Bram. 'We're hoping to stay a couple of nights.'

'No, that's all right,' the woman said. 'Pay us before you go. And if you want fresh eggs we've always got plenty.'

Mattie said hello to the baby, jiggling its chubby hand in hers. The little girl stared solemnly at her, then her face broke out in a wreath of smiles.

'She likes you.' The woman stared at Mattie. 'She don't usually take to strangers.'

Mattie felt strangely pleased. She had never liked babies much but this angel-child with fair hair and blue eyes had captured her heart. She put her hands over her face then took them away quickly. 'Peek-a-boo,' she said and the child burst into a peal of chuckles.

Bram was grinning all over his face. 'That always makes them laugh,' he said.

Mattie grinned at him. 'Oh, you know all about babies, do you?'

Bram went red. 'Only from my mate, you know, Tom. His mum had a baby last year.'

Mattie jiggled the baby's fingers again.

'We'd better go,' Bram said. 'We want to find the house before it gets dark.'

'Are you looking for somewhere in particular?' the farmer's wife asked curiously.

Bram and Mattie exchanged glances. Bram raised his eyebrows and shrugged as if to say sorry.

Mattie dragged a piece of paper from her back pocket. It really didn't matter if the woman knew where they were going. It was only a habit she'd picked up from Mary, not wanting anyone to know her business. 'Lilac Avenue,' she said. 'Any idea where it is?'

'Oh, yes. It's just behind the park . . . runs adjacent to it, actually. Go through the town and turn right at the roundabout . . . it's about the second or third turning on the left. Nice old Victorian houses.'

'That sounds like it. Thanks,' Mattie said relieved, nevertheless, when the woman didn't ask any more questions.

'Sorry,' Bram said when they were driving down the steep hill towards the town. 'I didn't mean to give the game away.'

Mattie put her hand on his knee. 'It's OK. It really doesn't matter.'

Mattie was determined not to become like Mary. Mary had never talked about her private life to anyone. It had taken ages before she trusted Katherine, or James . . . or any of them for that matter.

'I seem to spend half my life trying *not* to be like my mum,' she said.

Bram grinned at her. 'And all you've succeeded in doing is being very trying.'

'Do shut up.' She giggled and punched his arm. If everyone in the world was like Bram, she thought, there'd be no need not to trust anyone. Although . . . she frowned. She'd never really thought of it before. What reason did her mum have to be so suspicious about people? Maybe, now, she would never know.

'Where did you learn to do that with kids?' Bram asked. He hooted at a cyclist wobbling in front of them.

'What?'

'That peep-bo stuff.'

'People do it all the time to babies, dumb head. And anyway—'

'What?'

He took his eyes off the road and glanced at her. Mattie fiddled with her thumbnail. 'That's what *they* do.'

'Who?'

'My people . . . the people I see.'

'The ghosties?'

Mattie couldn't help laughing. 'They're not ghosties . . . I told you.'

27

'Sorry,' Bram said. 'Go on . . .'

'They come up really close and put their hands over their faces—' She couldn't go on. It sounded really daft.

Bram was suddenly serious. 'Mattie, I really worry about these . . . these people.'

'There's no need, honestly.' She leaned across and kissed him. It was better to make light of it. That's what she would do in future. Treat it as a bit of a joke. 'And I'm not a nut case, honestly.'

'Are you sure? The last thing I want to do is go camping with a nut case.'

Mattie punched him again. 'It takes one to know one,' she said lightly.

Bram grinned but his eyes were still serious. 'Whatever you say, captain.'

Mattie was glad when the roundabout loomed ahead.

'Turn right here,' she said. She looked down at the address on her bit of paper. She suddenly felt apprehensive. It would seem really strange, coming face to face with the house where her mother had been brought up. The house her grandparents had lived in. The house that belonged to her. An image suddenly came into her head. A wide bay window with lace curtains; an aspidistra sitting on top of a piano.

Bram changed gear and swung round the roundabout. They drove alongside the tree-lined public park. A wide stretch of green with swings and a pond in the middle. To one side rose a tree-covered mound with wooden picnic tables and benches.

Mattie suddenly grabbed Bram's arm. Her heart thudded. There was something about this place . . .

'Bram, stop . . . please!'

4

The Mini screeched to a halt by the kerb. 'What is it, Mattie?'

But Mattie couldn't speak. Her heart was still hammering. Frowning, she opened the door and got out as if she was in a dream.

'Mattie?'

Bram's voice receded into the distance. Mattie walked across the green towards the pond. There were a few ducks swimming idly about looking bored. As she got near the bank they swam rapidly towards her jostling each other as if there was no space instead of that great mass of water all to themselves. All of a sudden she had a vision of herself leaning forward and throwing something . . . a great big piece of bread . . . so big she could hardly hold it. A whole loaf . . . ?

Bram caught up with her.

'Mattie, what is it?'

She turned to him, her eyes shining. 'Bram, I *have* been here before, I'm absolutely positive. I remember feeding the ducks with a huge bit of bread.' She gazed round. 'And I remember having a picnic up there . . . under the trees.'

She ran forward and up the slope. She stood between two oak trees and looked back. The park had been full of people. So many you could hardly find a place to sit. There had been a crowd of kids round a Punch and Judy man by the pavilion and in the distance a fairground sang and whirled bright lights in the afternoon. A Mr Whippy van had been parked by the pond. It must have been here. Surely no other place could be exactly like this?

'Mattie, are you sure?' Bram was looking worried again. Mattie wasn't surprised. She was behaving like a maniac.

She sat down on the grass and pulled him down with her. She put her arms round her knees and sat hugging them tightly. She gazed out over the pond.

'Yes.' She was as sure as she had ever been about anything in her life. 'There's no doubt about it, Bram. My mum definitely brought me here. I don't know when but I know she did.'

Bram pulled at a bit of grass and stuck it between his front teeth. 'Mattie, we've got to find out what this is all about.'

She gazed at him. Her brain was whirling. 'Yes.'

He stood up. 'Come on, let's find this house of yours. Maybe you'll remember being there too?'

'Right.'

In an odd way, Mattie hoped so too. It might simply mean that Mary did bring her here as a child. That the quarrel with her parents took place after Mattie was born. Yes, she decided. That was definitely it. Mary had said her parents were old fashioned. They'd quarrelled over something and Mary had left, never to return. She had changed her name so they'd never find her. It was all, really, quite simple. Although why Mary had felt the need to lie to her when it was all over and done with, she would never know.

She sat back in the seat feeling better.

Lilac Avenue was the next turning.

'Number six,' Mattie said, nervous again. Her heart was right up in her throat. She pointed. 'Here, on the right.'

They pulled up outside a tall, Victorian house. Its dark red bricks were sombre in the dying sunlight. The wide bay windows were heavily shrouded with lace. A yellow rose clambered over the porch, almost covering the stained-glass panels on either side. A tub of geraniums stood guard by the blue-painted front door.

Mattie drew in her breath. She loved old places. Thatched cottages, farm houses, medieval timbered houses. Houses where ordinary folk had lived and squabbled amongst themselves, cooked and slept and made love. If

30

she ever went inside one she seemed to feel their presence all around her. She imagined she could hear their voices . . . children playing, the crashing of pots and pans.

She hated stately homes that were nothing but mausoleums full of the souvenirs of rich, dead people. Places you were herded around like sheep not daring to touch or hardly even breathe. She never felt anything there, only a sense of unreality. She liked *real* houses, where *real* people had lived.

Mattie stood and gazed at number six, Lilac Avenue. It must be one of the loveliest houses she had ever seen. She also knew, without any shadow of doubt, that she had never been here before in her life.

Beside her, Bram gasped. 'Wow! I didn't expect anything as posh as this.'

'No,' said Mattie with a tremor in her voice. 'Neither did I.'

Bram was looking at her. 'Well . . . recognize it?'

Mattie shook her head. 'No, definitely not.'

They sat staring at the house in silence. There was no sign of any activity. Next door, a curtain twitched then fell back into place. A boy whizzed past on a skateboard and veered off across the road and into the park.

'Do they know you're coming?' Bram asked.

'No.' Mattie unzipped her bag. 'But I've brought a letter from the solicitor proving who I am.'

'Good thinking, Batman,' Bram said. He took the keys out of the ignition. 'Come on then, Mattie. Once more unto the breach . . .'

She suddenly felt her stomach churn with apprehension. 'Bram, I'm not sure if I really want to—'

He stared at her. 'Come on, Mattie.'

She struggled to pull herself together. This was crazy. Since when did Mattie Browne admit she was scared of things? She'd always had to be the strong one. Especially with Mary hardly wanting to leave the house at times. Hurrying to work, hurrying home as if someone was chasing her, then shutting the curtains against the world before it even got dark.

She pushed open the car door. 'OK, I'm sorry.' That was another thing. She *had* to stop apologizing.

The gate hinge squeaked as Mattie pushed it open. The front path was made up of tiles, red and green in a pattern like diamonds. It led up to the front porch then on round the side of the house. Mattie's hand hovered over the bell. This is my house, she thought. My garden . . . it's really blowing my mind.

'Have you changed your mind?' Bram was asking.

'No, 'course not.' She pushed the bell determinedly. The clanging along the interior hallway brought no response. Mattie pushed it again.

Bram stood looking up, tapping the toe of his boot on the edge of the step. 'Nice gables,' he murmured.

'Shut up,' she giggled.

Her ears strained for the sound of footsteps. None came.

'There's no one in.' She turned, disappointed now she had finally plucked up courage to face whoever answered the door. 'We'll have to come back tomorrow.'

Then a voice came from round the side of the house. 'Just coming.'

A stocky, middle-aged man with a bald head appeared from the side gate. He held a pair of gardening shears. He looked suspiciously at the two young people on the doorstep. Mattie wondered what he would say when he knew the girl wearing the leather jacket and jeans actually owned the house. She couldn't help smiling to herself.

Mattie went forward and held out her hand. She was suddenly filled with confidence. There were no ghosts here. 'Hi,' she said brightly introducing herself.

'. . . and this is my friend, Bram. We wondered if it would be OK to take a look around. I've never actually been here before, you see.'

The man looked wary . . . as if they could be anybody . . . burglars . . . Jehovah's Witnesses . . . spies from the DSS.

Mattie took the letter out of her bag. 'Look,' she said. 'I've got a letter from Mrs Hodson, my solicitor. I really am Mary Browne's daughter.'

The man scanned it quickly. 'I'm sorry,' he said, looking relieved. 'We were notified of your mother's death and the fact that we had a new landlord. I'm so sorry. I just didn't expect you to be so young.'

'That's OK. Would it be all right to see the house now or shall we come back some other time?'

The man put the shears down on the side of the path. 'No, no, come on in. My wife's out at evening classes, I'm afraid, but I'll be glad to show you round.'

'Thanks.'

They followed him round the back of the house. The border was strewn with shrubs. Ahead, a long lawn stretched towards a wooden summerhouse. A hammock was slung between two apple trees. It moved slightly in the breeze as if rocked by some invisible hand. The scent of roses hung in the air. Mattie wondered if Mum had ever sat soaked in the perfume of the garden or swung in the hammock, daydreaming the world away.

'It's a lovely house,' Mattie said with a little shake in her voice. Bram gave her a quick glance then squeezed her hand. She gave him a grateful smile. 'It's much bigger than I thought it would be,' she continued.

'It's really too big for us,' the man said, ushering them into the kitchen. 'Both the kids have left home since we came here . . . we've been thinking about finding some-where smaller once the lease is up.'

'Yes,' Mattie said. She wasn't really listening. She was thinking about Mum, living in this beautiful house and never mentioning it.

'Who did the place up?' Bram was asking. His eyes roved the kitchen, through into the dining room. There was a long, pine table, a bookshelf full of paperbacks.

The man, who had introduced himself as Clive Armstrong, scratched his cheek and looked puzzled. 'Your mother,' he said, staring at Mattie. 'Well . . . not actually her, of course. She paid for the place to be stripped and renovated when the old lady died. Or so the agent told us.'

'Oh?' Mattie felt a fool, not knowing.

'Didn't you know?'

'No.' Mattie found herself wanting to change the subject. He would think it really weird she'd never even known of the existence of the place, let alone if it had been redecorated or not. 'Is it OK if we see the rest of the house?' she said quickly.

'Yes, sure . . .'

He took them on a guided tour. 'The windows are original,' he said, pointing out the wide bays with their small panes of stained glass at the top, 'and the fireplaces.'

'Was it in a bad state, then?' asked Bram, eyeing a pair of antique vases with interest.

Clive shook his head. 'Apparently not. This was the strange thing really. The agent told us the old couple kept it in really good nick. It was just—' he broke off.

'What?' They were upstairs in the bedroom and Mattie was gazing out over the back of the park. There was a gate through from the bottom of the garden. Two lads were kicking a ball against the fence. Had Mum ever stood in the same place . . . watching children play? Strangely, there was no atmosphere to the house, friendly or otherwise. It was as if it had all been eliminated, stripped with the wallpaper and thrown away.

'. . . nothing,' said Mr Armstrong. 'It's not for me to say.'

A voice came up the stairs. 'Clive, you up there?'

Mattie turned swiftly. 'What were you going to say?'

The man pressed his lips together. 'Well, apparently they tried to talk Mrs Browne out of renovating the place.'

'Miss . . .' Mattie interrupted although she didn't know why. It no longer mattered whether Mary was called Miss or Mrs or even Ms.

'Sorry?' Clive looked confused.

'Miss,' Mattie said. 'My mum was a Miss.'

'Oh, sorry. Anyway, she insisted it was gutted, apparently. Furniture, carpets . . . everything was sold and the place redecorated from top to bottom. Don't ask me why.'

By now there were footsteps coming up the stairs. 'My wife.' He wrung his hands together as if she had caught him doing something he shouldn't. He almost ran from the room. 'Up here, dear,' he called along the landing. They heard a hurried, whispered conversation.

'Are you still sure you've never been here?' hissed Bram, putting his hand on the waistband of Mattie's jeans.

'Positive,' she said. She was still staring out over the park. 'I wonder why Mum never came here?' she said almost to herself. 'Why did we live in the flat when we could have lived here?'

'Your mum's job, I suppose,' Bram said.

'She could have got a job anywhere,' Mattie said. 'Her boss told me she was the best secretary he'd ever had.'

A red-faced, red-haired woman in a green track suit came rushing into the room. She looked them both up and down as if two Hell's Angels had invaded her territory. Then she seemed to pull herself together. She held out her hand to Mattie.

'Miss Browne, I'm so sorry about—'

'That's OK,' said Mattie automatically. She supposed people felt they had to say that but she really wished they wouldn't. Especially people who hadn't known her mum from Adam.

'Would you like a cup of tea? Typical of Clive not to offer you one.'

Mattie shook her head. 'I'm all right, thanks.'

'Me too,' said Bram.

'Clive tells me you've never been to Porthland before.'

'No,' Mattie said flatly. God, it sounded so weird. Never visiting a house your mother had owned for six years . . . never visiting your grandparents in the whole of your life.

Mrs Armstrong waited for explanations but when none came she turned to her husband.

'Did you tell them about that box we found?'

He shook his head. 'Give me a chance, Jean. They've only been here five minutes.'

'What box?' asked Bram.

'In the airing cupboard,' explained the woman. 'The house clearance people must have missed it. It was tucked behind the tank. I suppose the old lady thought it would keep the stuff from getting damp.'

'What stuff?' Mattie came to.

'Oh, just old letters and bills . . . one or two photographs. I was going to throw them away but Clive said we should keep them. We thought the owner . . . well, you now, of course, Mattie, might come one day. We always thought it strange that your mother never came to see the house.'

The woman peered so closely at Mattie, Mattie half expected her to cover her face then say peek-a-boo.

'She . . . she was very busy,' said Mattie.

'Yes, I expect she was.' The woman turned to her husband. 'Go and get it, Clive.'

'Where is it?'

'You know very well where it is, now, Clive,' she said as if he was a naughty little boy. 'It's in the cupboard in the spare room.'

'Oh, yes . . . yes.' Clive went off mumbling to himself.

Mrs Armstrong took Mattie's arm. 'I'm so glad we kept it. Were you fond of your grandparents, dear?'

Mattie threw a despairing glance at Bram. Help, she thought. Rescue me from this witch.

'I like the stained glass,' Bram said in a loud voice as he followed them down the stairs. 'My dad and I are in the antiques business. It's quite rare to find original stuff still in houses these days.'

They waited in the hall as Clive came down the stairs with a cardboard box in his arms. 'Here you are,' he said, dumping it on the hall table. 'No family jewels, I'm afraid, but you might find the stuff interesting.'

'Thanks,' said Mattie. She couldn't wait to get the box back to the campsite. Maybe there would be a few answers inside.

'Are you sure you won't stay for a cup of tea?' Clive's hand hovered near the kettle.

'They said no.' His wife frowned at him.

'Thanks anyway,' Mattie said hastily.

Clive went with them to the door.

'You're not going to put the rent up, are you?' he said jovially.

Mattie didn't even know how much the rent was.

'I shouldn't have thought so,' she said.

'Are you likely to move in here yourself one day?' Clive hovered on the doorstep as if he didn't want them to go.

Mattie looked up at the bedroom windows. 'I don't know,' she said. 'One day, maybe.'

They had supper—an unhealthy fry-up. Eggs from the farm, bacon, sausages, beans . . . stuff they'd brought from home. All cooked together in one pan.

Then Mattie opened the box.

It was a balmy evening. Breezes drifted lazily in from the ocean. From somewhere across the fields a curlew called plaintively, its voice sounding as if it searched for lost souls.

Mattie and Bram sat outside on camping stools. A flutter of moths kamikazied against the hissing gas lamp. So many were dying Mattie wanted to turn it out. Instead, Bram rigged up a kind of umbrella affair with a tea cloth over the top so the moths shouldn't hit the hot glass. The sound of rock music thumped from one of the other tents. Two shadows swayed in time to the beat, the figures distorted and made mysterious by the flicker of the lamp within.

'Well?' Bram stacked the dishes into their box. 'Aren't you going to look inside?'

Mattie realized then that she had been putting it off. She

gazed towards the cliff top. There were two people there. Her people. The man. The woman. The man turned. Smiled. Waved. Then they both disappeared from view.

A shiver ran down Mattie's spine. For the first time in years she began to question their presence. She began to wonder exactly who they were. Or if, in fact, they were anybody. Yet she knew they weren't hallucinations. They were there in her mind's eye. Real. Maybe they *were* ghosts after all. Ghosts who, for some reason best known to themselves, had chosen her and her alone to haunt. Or could they be people from another time whose lives had somehow got mixed up with hers? Or people from another dimension? It sounded like something out of *Star Trek*. *Aliens on the starboard bow, Captain*. Only they weren't aliens. This man, this woman, these ghosts, these friends, whether she liked it or not, were part of Mattie's life.

Bram was passing his hand in front of her face. He peered at her. 'Is anyone there?'

Mattie came to. 'Sorry, I was miles away.' She was going to tell him they'd been there but then changed her mind. What was the point? Bram couldn't see them. No one else could. They were hers. Entirely hers.

'Shall I do it for you?'

She could see he was dying of curiosity.

'Go on then.'

A few old letters and bills, Clive Armstrong had said. Mattie didn't really suppose there would be any answers in those.

The first thing of real interest was a photograph of Mary. She looked about eighteen.

'It was taken at Lilac Avenue,' Bram pointed out. He looked on the back for writing. There wasn't any.

Mattie was staring at it. Her eyes filled and she brushed the moisture away. 'She hardly looks any different, does she?' Bram must have heard the catch in her voice. He put his arm round her and pulled his camp stool closer. 'From when she was well, I mean,' Mattie continued.

It seemed a lifetime ago . . . Mum being well.

'No.' Bram covered her hand with his. 'We'll leave it if it upsets you.'

Mattie shook her head and brushed the back of her hand across her face. She took the photo from him. 'No. It's just weird, that's all. I know it's silly but I always had this strange idea that because there were no pictures of her when she was young, that she wasn't ever young at all, if you see what I mean?'

She looked, bright eyed, at Bram. He grinned. 'Yes, I think I do.'

Mattie held the picture up to the lamp. Her mother was wearing sensible brown lace-up shoes and a plain dress buttoned right up to the neck. She was staring awkwardly at the camera as if she hated having her picture taken even then. Her hair was much fairer than Mattie remembered. Once, it had been almost black, like Mattie's. But then Mary had let the dye grow out. Mattie remembered being really surprised that her mother was really fair when she had thought her so dark.

'You're not a bit like her, Mattie.'

'No,' Mattie said. 'I've always thought I must be like my father. Whoever he was.'

Then there was another picture. A photograph of two older people. A man and a woman.

Mattie drew in her breath. Her grandparents . . . they'd got to be. The woman looked just like Mary. Both people glared sternly at the camera as if they were about to tell the holder off. The man held a bible. It was open in his hand as if he was just about to burst forth into a sermon about hell and damnation and the terrible sins of the human race.

'Wow,' Bram said. 'He looks a bit of a tyrant.'

'Yes,' said Mattie. 'He was.'

'You don't recognize them?'

Mattie shook her head. 'No. Not at all. I've never even seen a picture of them. I did ask Mum once but she just said she didn't have any.'

39

'It's funny. You remember being in the park but never going to the house or meeting these . . .' He turned the picture over. 'Matilda and Frederick.' Bram looked at her. 'Did you know that was their names?'

'No,' Mattie said. She dropped her gaze then looked at him from beneath lowered eyelids. He was staring at her. His mouth slowly stretched into a broad, knowing grin.

Mattie felt herself go red. 'Don't say anything, Bram,' she threatened, 'or I'll kill you, honestly I will.'

'Mattie . . . Matilda.' Bram's eyes twinkled with mischief. He clapped his hand to his forehead. 'Don't tell me I've fallen in love with someone called Matilda!'

Mattie picked up her Coke can and threw it at him. He fell back off the stool, long legs waving in the air.

'Shut *up*, Bram!' She tried to be annoyed but couldn't help laughing too.

Mattie had been seven or eight before she learned her name was Matilda. Then she had been too embarrassed to tell anyone, even Bram, her best friend since childhood. Luckily, people had simply taken it for granted her name was just Mattie. At least, now, she knew why her mother had chosen such an old-fashioned name for her only child. But the oddest thing of all was that Mum hadn't told her she was named for the grandmother she never knew. The whole thing was crazy.

Bram was still rolling on the grass and laughing his head off.

He crawled over to Mattie and buried his head in her lap. 'I'm sorry,' he said. 'I shouldn't laugh.'

'No,' she said, still grinning. 'You shouldn't.' Mattie banged him on the head with the photograph. 'Get up, idiot.'

Bram wiped his hand around his face. 'Why didn't you tell me?'

'Why do you *think*?' she said.

Bram picked up his stool and sat down close to her. 'OK, Matilda.'

'Bram!'

He held up his hands. 'Sorry, sorry, sorry.'

'You solemnly promise never to tell anyone.' She squeezed his bicep as hard as she could.

'Ow! Yes, I promise. Scout's honour. I'll never tell anyone your real name's Matilda.' He snorted. 'You'll have to keep your birth certificate under wraps.'

'I don't even know where it is.'

Bram sobered up at last. 'It'll be with your mum's things, I expect.'

'Yes,' Mattie said. 'I expect so.'

'Let's see what else we've got.'

But there seemed to be nothing else of great interest. A few old bills and receipts. An old medical card of Mattie's mother's. There was a letter from a woman named Amy Dray giving one week's notice from her job. It was addressed to Mattie's grandmother.

'Looks as if she was a cleaning lady or something,' Mattie said. She tucked the letter back into its envelope. Inside there was another, smaller envelope as if it had slipped in by mistake. Mattie recognized her mother's handwriting straight away.

She quickly scanned the words. She was good at that . . . reading quickly, absorbing information at first glance. But this time she had to read it again, more slowly the second time.

'Look at this,' she croaked. She handed the letter to Bram. He read out loud.

'Dear Mother and Father,

By the time you get this letter I shall be miles away. Although you have not been aware of it, I have met and fallen in love with a young man. We met last year when he came for the Carnival with Saracen's Fun-fair. Now he has come back and has asked me to go away with him. It would be easy for you to find me and try to bring me back but please don't. I know you will feel ashamed that I have run away with someone you will

41

*consider to be a common fairground worker but I love
him and he loves me.*

Mary

'Oh, God, Mattie!' Bram stared at her in horror.

Mattie's finger shook as she pointed to the date on the letter. 'See that,' she said, hardly able to believe her eyes. '19th August, 1978.'

'Oh my God!' Bram looked more shocked than ever. 'That's your birthday!'

Mattie couldn't sleep that night. She lay, wide awake. She could feel the gentle rise and fall of Bram's chest as he slept beside her. His arm was thrown across her chest and now and then he murmured something in his sleep.

Through the open flap Mattie could see the stars. They looked so clear she felt that if she stretched out her hand she could almost touch them. She wondered if *they* might come. For the first time in her life she tried to make them . . . tried to conjure them up out of thin air. They seemed, besides Bram, to be the only thing she could be sure of. Everything else seemed to be falling about her ears. Her mother, Mary Browne, hadn't been Mary Browne at all but Mary Hughes. Her grandparents were dead but hadn't died when she thought they had. Her father . . . was he some dark-haired fairground man and not just some bloke Mum had met on holiday? And now she couldn't have been born when her mother said she had been born at all. She wasn't even the *age* she thought she was. How could that be, she thought? It was crazy, mind-blowing, ridiculous. She felt her eyes brim. The whole thing was a nightmare.

'We'll find your birth certificate when we get back,' Bram had said, trying to comfort her.

Mattie gently removed Bram's arm and crawled from the tent. The moon was high and full. The sky a deep, dark navy, polka-dotted with stars. Mattie walked to the edge of the cliff and leaned on the fence. Out to sea, the lights of a passing cargo ship winked on the horizon. Below, waves hammered the cliff base with a noise like thunder. Mattie sat on the grass and clasped her hands round her knees. She shivered then pulled the baggy T-shirt she wore as a nightie down over her knees as far as it would go.

What are you supposed to do when your whole life turns out to be a lie? It was as if she had covered her face with her hands and when she took them away she had inexplicably become someone else. She had changed from Mattie Browne into Matilda Hughes. Or had she? Maybe she couldn't even be certain of that?

Then she heard the swish and pad of footsteps on the grass. Bram was behind her.

'Mattie! You scared me.' He pulled her to her feet and held her close. 'Don't do that, OK?'

'I'm sorry.' She realized she was shivering. Her feet and legs were bare and the night was chilly.

'Come back to the tent, Mattie. You'll catch your death.'

Two deaths in two weeks . . .

Mattie looked up as they walked back. They were there, either side of the tent flap in the light from the glimmering lamp. They beckoned. Smiled.

Mattie stopped. 'Who *are* you?' she called out loud.

She looked at Bram but it was clear he could see nothing.

And when she looked back they had gone.

5

'I wonder,' Bram said next morning, 'if that woman, what was her name? Amy something or other. The one who wrote the letter to your grandma, giving in her notice . . .'

'Amy Dray,' said Mattie. 'What about her?'

Mattie was folding up the sleeping bag. She felt groggy, still half asleep. She had lain awake for hours. She didn't know what time it was when she eventually dozed off. All she knew was that it had begun to get light. Even then she'd tossed and turned and kept thinking she heard Mum call out to her as she used to so often during those long dark nights of her illness.

'I wonder if she still lives here?' Bram was saying.

'Mrs Thingie . . . so what if she does?'

'She might be able to tell you something about your mum.'

Mattie yawned. 'What kind of thing?'

Bram shrugged. 'I dunno . . . something that might explain the mix up with the dates.' He spread his hands. 'You've got to find out what went on, Mattie. I just thought it might help to talk to someone who knew the family. I mean if your mum was pregnant when she left . . .'

'Don't be daft.' Mattie snapped at him then immediately felt guilty. Bram was only doing all this for her sake. 'She wouldn't have given birth to me the day she left home, would she?' she went on more softly. 'You can't hide the fact you're pregnant for nine months, you know.'

'You do read about that sometimes. Someone just going into labour and thinking they've got stomach ache.'

She looked at him scornfully. 'And you believe it?'

He shrugged, then grinned. 'No, not really. But, Mattie . . . it's just all so weird.'

'I know. I've been thinking about it all night.' Remembering lying awake, everything going round and round in her brain, triggered the tears. Bram put his arm round her neck and held her until she stopped.

'I'm sorry,' she croaked, annoyed with herself. 'I'm such a wimp.'

'No, you're not. You've had enough to cope with. Still want to look at that letter?'

Mattie sniffed. ' 'Course.'

Mattie pulled out the box from under the folding table. She rummaged through. 'Yes, here it is,' she said. '14th January, 1979.' She looked at him. 'That could mean she worked for them at the time Mum ran away.'

'What's the address?' Bram peered over her shoulder.

Mattie read it out.

'We could go and see her.'

'Do you reckon she'll still be there after all this time?'

Bram shrugged. 'There's only one way to find out.'

'It would be better to ring,' Mattie said.

A coward's way, she thought. Easier than coming face to face with another bit of Mary's past she hadn't known existed. Maybe even a bit of her own.

'OK.'

But Mattie still felt doubtful. Was there really any point in dragging it all up? Bram must have seen the uncertainty on her face.

'Come on, Mattie,' he said. 'We might as well find out as much as we can while we're here. It'll be twice as hard once we get back.' He toyed with her fingers. 'Mattie, I know you . . . you'll never be able to think about anything else until you know the truth.'

But Mattie still wasn't really positive she *wanted* to know. Whatever reason Mum had for telling her those fibs . . . they must have been good ones. Perhaps it would be better to let sleeping dogs lie?

'Well?' Bram was waiting patiently for an answer.

She shrugged. He was right, as usual. She'd never rest

until she knew the whole story. 'OK, if you want.'

'No, Mattie. If *you* want.'

'Right,' she said, smiling. '*I* want.'

The nearest phone box was over a kilometre away. Mattie could hardly hear what the enquiry operator was saying for the roar of holiday traffic heading for the beach. It was a baking hot day. Mirages rose from the tarmac even though it was only ten o'clock in the morning.

Mattie came out waving her little notebook. 'Got it,' she said. 'She still lives there.'

'Great,' Bram said from the driving seat of the Mini. 'Are you going to phone then?'

'I haven't got any more change.'

Bram fumbled in his jeans pocket. 'Neither have I. Come on, we'll get some in town.'

They were lucky to find a parking space down by the harbour. Mattie bought ice lollies. They sat on the sea wall, sucking like mad before the lollies melted and made orange streaks down their arms. Then Mattie went to phone Amy Dray.

Her heart was hammering as she dialled. What on earth was she going to say? The woman would probably think she was mad. She might not even remember Mum.

Amy's husband answered. He had a deep, soft, Cornish accent. Mattie hesitantly explained who she was and he went off to find his wife.

Mattie tapped her fingers impatiently on the glass. It was like an oven inside the phone box. She felt as if she was being cooked. She could see Bram, sitting on the sea wall swinging his long legs. He was watching a group of sun-bronzed children building a sand castle. Did Mum ever come down here to build castles in the sand? Somehow Mattie doubted it. By the stern look on her grandfather's face he thought anything so trivial as castle building was a sin.

Mattie jumped when a hesitant voice in her ear said, 'Hello? This is Amy Dray.'

Mattie told her who she was.

'Oh, my.' The woman sounded quite stunned. 'Mary Hughes's daughter . . . I never would have believed it.'

'You remember her?' Mattie said, her heart still dancing its wild beat.

'Of course I remember her. In fact that was one reason why I left the Hughes's employ. It was miserable working at Lilac Avenue without Mary there. I'm so sorry to hear she died, dear.'

'Yes,' said Mattie.

'How did you find me?' Amy asked. 'I mean there's none of the family left now.'

Mattie explained about the letter.

'Well, well,' the woman said again. 'What a funny thing to keep.'

'There were lots of old letters and bills,' Mattie said. 'They were the only things left after the house in Lilac Avenue had been cleared out.'

'I remember Mary so well,' said Amy and her voice took on a dreamy, far away sound as people's voices do when they're remembering the past. 'We were good pals in spite of the age difference. She didn't have any friends of her own age. Sweet thing she was, very quiet and shy.'

'I . . . I wondered if she ever told you anything about a man from the fair,' Mattie asked hesitantly.

There was silence for a minute. 'What man was that then, dear?'

'Well, you see I'm trying to find out why Mum left home. I wondered if she went away with someone from the fun-fair.'

Mattie could have kicked herself for saying that. It sounded crazy. Why on earth should Mattie think something like that unless someone had told her.

'Is that what she told you?' Amy's voice sounded cautious.

Mattie could tell the woman only half believed her. 'Er . . . kind of,' she fibbed. She bit her lip. She hated telling lies.

She heard Amy sigh.

'I'm afraid I don't know anything about that, dear. Saracen's fair *does* come here every year but I don't remember Mary ever going to it. Mr and Mrs Hughes said she had gone to London to live with an aunt. I must say I thought it odd at the time, her just up and leaving like that. But that's what they said and they weren't people to tell fibs, you know.'

'No,' Mattie said.

'I just assumed she'd got a good job in London. She didn't have a Cornish accent at all, you see. Going to that boarding school and everything.'

'No,' Mattie said. That was something else she didn't know. Mary had been away at boarding school. She shook her head. What else was she going to find out?

Mattie couldn't bring herself to ask outright if Mrs Dray knew if Mum had been pregnant when she left. It seemed a daft question anyway, in view of what Amy had already told her.

'She didn't talk about him, then?' Mattie said.

'Who, dear?'

'The man from the fair,' Mattie repeated patiently.

'Oh, no. Not to me, anyway. Mary wasn't one to go out with men though. And even if she had been, she certainly would never have been allowed to associate with anyone from the fairground.'

'No,' Mattie said. 'I suppose not.'

'She was too shy and too afraid of her father. Very religious he was . . . her mother as well. Didn't approve of boyfriends and pop music and the like.'

That was that then. Mum had been right. Her parents had been ashamed to tell anyone the truth.

'Can you remember *when* she left home?' Mattie was aware she was asking a lot.

'You mean the *exact* date?'

'Um . . . if you can.'

'I'm sorry,' Amy said. 'I only remember it was around carnival time . . . oh, and 1978 of course.'

Of course, Mattie thought. The year I was supposed to be born. But how could that be? How could it possibly be?

'You're sure it was 1978?' Mattie said.

'Yes, positive, dear.'

'Well thanks, Mrs Dray,' Mattie said lamely even though her brain was whirling.

'I'm sorry I couldn't be of more help, my dear.'

'No . . .' Mattie hastened to assure her. 'You've been great. Thanks.'

Mattie heard a voice in the background. 'Who're you talking to, Ma?'

'Mattie Hughes.'

'No,' said Mattie. 'Mattie Browne.'

'Browne? Oh, Mary's married name, of course. I'm so pleased she had a daughter. She loved children so much. She used to spend hours sitting in the park, just watching the babies in their prams. I used to feel sad for her, thinking she'd never be likely to have one of her own. It just shows how wrong you can be, doesn't it?'

Mattie didn't bother explaining. There didn't seem to be any point.

'Any joy?' Bram asked as she came out.

'Not really.' Mattie was still trying to work out the puzzle. 'She thought Mum went away to live with an aunt in London.'

'Is that what they told everyone?'

'Looks like it.' She looked up at him. 'But she said it was definitely 1978. She was really positive about that.' Mattie shook her head. 'But she must be wrong, Bram. It must have been some other year. She must have got mixed up. By the sound of her she's getting on a bit.'

'She didn't say if your mum was pregnant when she left?'

'I didn't ask. Anyway, Mrs Dray said she'd never had anything to do with men.' Mattie sighed. 'Maybe I was a virgin birth?'

Bram grinned. 'You could make a fortune.'

She looked at him bleakly. 'I don't want a fortune. I just want to know what went on.'

'I know,' Bram said gently. 'OK, Mattie. Where do we go from here?'

'You tell me.'

Suddenly she was fed up with the whole thing. She slipped her hand into his. 'Let's go for a swim. We'll think about it again later, huh.'

They found a vacant spot on the beach and spread their towels. 'You go,' Mattie said content to watch for the time being. 'I'll come in a minute.'

She watched Bram stroll down the sand meandering in and out of the sunbathers. He stopped once to apologize for almost treading on someone's bag. Mattie smiled to herself then lay back and let the sun caress her. She stretched out, soaking it up like a thirsty sponge. She turned over on her stomach. Restlessly, she sat up again and covered herself with sun lotion then dragged her Walkman from her bag. She put in her favourite tape. Wild rock blared into her eardrums. It shut out the sound of the waves ... of children screaming ... the world.

'Ouch ... Bram!' He'd come back and shaken freezing drops of ocean water over her shiny limbs. She wrenched out the headphones and threw the tube of sun tan lotion at him. He laughed and grabbed the towel, rubbing his long hair with both hands until it stood up around his head like a halo. He plonked down beside her. 'Aren't you going in?'

She put her hand on the cool flesh of his thigh. 'What's it like?'

Bram tossed his hair out of his eyes. 'Er ... well, it's cold and blue and once you manage to get past all the pollution, quite clean.'

'Twit.'

She punched his stomach and jumped to her feet. She couldn't resist the thought of the water cooling her sun-warmed skin. She skipped down the beach. The warm sand was like oil between her toes. She splashed along the shallows for a little way. Children basked in the warm water like baby seals. Along by the rocks it was less crowded. Mattie liked the thought of having a whole ocean to herself.

She waded out then dived under. She gasped as the first cold shock took away her breath. She swam parallel with the shore for a little way then she bobbed up, turned and swam strongly out to sea. Two boys in an inflatable dinghy shouted and waved. She trod water, waving back. A helicopter flew across the ocean surface. There was a man sitting in the open doorway taking photographs. Mattie waved at him too.

She looked back towards the beach. The sand was dotted with colour as if the desert had bloomed. She swam back, feeling for the sand beneath her feet. She shook the water from her face and waded towards the shore. Moisture gathered in droplets and ran from her oiled skin. The sea lapped around her, shimmering as the sun hit the water.

They were sitting where a rocky outcrop cut the beach in two. Although the images were blurred, indistinct, Mattie could see that the woman wore a sundress . . . green cotton with shoestring straps. The man had shorts on and a polo shirt, clumsy brown sandals with black socks. They had all the paraphernalia of holidaymakers spending the day on the beach. A picnic basket, and big plastic beach bag . . . a beach ball. The woman was waving a tiny hat and shouting something. The man took the hat from her and began walking towards Mattie. Then the images wavered and disappeared altogether. Mattie frowned. It was the first time she had ever seen them *with* anything. Usually it was just them . . . and their hands . . . and their smile.

She waited. Maybe they would come back? For some strange reason she needed desperately to see them. When they didn't she felt a sudden rapid uneven heartbeat of panic. What if she never saw them again? What if, like Mum, they had gone for ever? Inexplicably she began to tremble. She hugged herself for warmth even though the sun was beginning to burn her naked shoulders. She was suddenly overcome by blind terror. Something . . . someone had been taken away from her and she would never see them again. Of course . . . Mum. She tried to pull herself together but that scary, black feeling of dread just wouldn't go away. She stood, taking frantic gulps of air. Her eyes flew to and fro along the shore, searching. But all she could see were the myriads of tourists . . . children playing . . . people trying to push baby buggies across the sand . . . and all she could hear were the seagulls crying overhead and the diminishing noise of the helicopter, its blades thumping the hot, noon-day air like a distant drum.

Suddenly she needed Bram more than she had ever needed anything else in her life.

She stumbled to the shore then sped along the sea's edge. Tears streamed down her face. People stared, dodged out of her way.

'Bram!' she yelled at the top of her voice.

In the distance she saw him sit up then push himself up off the sand and begin running towards her.

She stretched out her arms as he reached her and laid her head, sobbing, on his shoulder. His arms were round her, so tight she knew she couldn't fall down even if she wanted to.

'Mattie . . . Mattie?' She could tell she had scared him.

She shook her head. 'Oh, Bram, I'm sorry.' Why was she always apologizing?

He led her gently back to their place on the sand.

'Is she OK?' a man with a little child asked. His face was full of concern.

'She'll be fine,' Bram explained. 'Her mum's just died . . . I don't think it's really hit her before.'

Bram sat her down and held her until she stopped shaking. He wiped her face with the edge of the towel then had to brush sand from round her nose.

'What happened, Mattie?'

She shook her head and drew her hand across her eyes. 'I had a panic attack. God, I'm sorry, Bram. I'm getting as bad as Mum.'

'Hey,' Bram wiped the moisture from her cheeks with his thumbs. 'Don't say that.'

'I saw my people,' she went on. 'They were sitting on a rock.'

'Is that what upset you?'

She shook her head. 'I don't know. They disappeared and I just had this terrible feeling of panic . . . as if everything I loved had suddenly deserted me.'

'It must be because of your mum.'

'I suppose so. God, Bram. I'm such a fool. You know I've felt guilty because I was *pleased* when she died. Actually *pleased* because she wasn't in pain any more.'

'There's nothing wrong with that, Mattie.'

'No, I suppose not. But why should seeing those people make me feel like that. I never have before . . . they've always been like friends.'

'You've seen them here before, haven't you?'

She might have guessed he'd known.

'Yes,' she said. She sniffed. She felt better . . . strangely purged. Everyone knows that it's good to let your emotions out but she still didn't understand the panic attack. She'd had one once before. But that was years ago when she'd woken to find the flat empty. Mary had only popped next door to borrow something but Mattie remembered that terrible feeling of being abandoned as if it was yesterday.

Bram bit his lip. 'Mattie . . . I think you should see someone.'

'You mean you think I've got problems like Mum had?' She stared at him panic stricken.

'No, I don't mean that, Mattie. I told you, you're the

sanest person I know. But . . .' He took her hand, played with her fingers gently as if they were something delicate and might break. Like one of his precious antiques. He didn't look at her. 'I've been thinking about it a lot,' he said seriously. 'I really don't believe your people are ghosties, or spirits or anything like that. I reckon they could be people in your memory . . . people you knew when you were a kid.'

'Then I'd know who they were, wouldn't I?'

'Not necessarily. I've been reading a bit about childhood amnesia. You know, things that happened to us when we were kids but the memories are buried in our subconscious.'

'Where did you read that?'

'I remembered Mum did a psychology course at college once. I dug out one of her old books. It said that sometimes those subconscious memories come to the surface and that's when we get feelings of *déjà vu* and that kind of stuff.'

'I read about that too,' Mattie said. 'But I didn't connect it with what happens to me.'

'I called a mate of mine too. His dad's into all this alternative stuff. He does hypnotism. I read that you can bring these hidden memories to the surface under hypnosis.'

'Oh,' Mattie said again. She wasn't sure she liked Bram talking about her to a stranger. And she wasn't sure she liked the idea of hypnosis either. Giving your subconscious over to someone was really scary. 'Why didn't you tell me this before?'

'I thought you'd got enough on your plate.' He gazed at her and she could tell he hadn't been sure what her reaction would be. 'Don't worry,' he added hastily. 'I didn't mention your name or anything.'

Mattie felt guilty. As usual, Bram had known what she was thinking.

'I don't know why I hadn't thought of it before.'

'Maybe you didn't really want to know?'

Mattie dropped her gaze. 'No, I don't think it's that. I think I had enough of that kind of stuff with Mum and all.

54

I thought one person having therapy in the family was enough.'

'They're not the same . . . shrinks and hypnotists.'

'I know that, twit. But it's never worried me that I see my people. They've just been part of my life like . . .' she had a job to think of a comparison, 'like a pet dog or something that follows you about.'

'But they worry you now.'

She shrugged. 'They don't *worry* me exactly. I'm just beginning to want to know who they are . . . or were.'

'I've been thinking about something else as well,' Bram said.

She dried herself then rubbed in some more sun cream. She felt back to normal, a bit of a fraud that she had panicked over nothing. 'Your brain must ache.'

He grinned and lay down with his face up to the sun. 'My brain always aches.'

She laughed. 'Go on.'

'Well . . .' Bram ran his hand across his face as he always did when upset, or angry, or didn't know how to put something. He turned towards her and leaned on one elbow. '*Where* were you born, Mattie?'

'Up north somewhere.'

'Yes, but where up north?'

Mattie shrugged. 'Near Yorkshire, Mum always said.'

'You don't know exactly?'

'No.'

'Well, your birth certificate will tell you where you were registered.'

'Registered?' said Mattie.

'Yes, births have to be registered same as deaths.'

Mattie squeezed his arm. 'I know that, stupid. But does it have to be the place you were born in?'

'I suppose so. The nearest town anyway.'

'Right.' Mattie brightened up. 'So that's not a problem. We'll know where Mum went with the guy from the fair.'

'If they stayed together.'

'Hm. I suppose she could have got pregnant then they split up.'

'It happens all the time,' Bram said.

'I can't think why she told me she had an affair with a stranger, though. Surely it would have been better to tell me my dad was someone she loved. That's what most people would do.'

'Your mum wasn't like *most* people.'

'Don't I know it,' Mattie said ruefully.

Bram drew patterns on her arm with his sandy fingertip. 'Try not to worry, Mattie. I'm sure there's a simple explanation.'

'I wish I was.'

She leaned down and kissed him on the forehead. She couldn't help it. He looked so earnest, so eager to get the matter cleared up so she could get on with her life. His skin was damp and tasted salty. 'You know when I first read that letter I felt relieved.'

'How do you mean?'

'Well . . .' Mattie scooped a palmful of sand and let it run slowly through her fingers like the flowing of time through an hourglass. 'I could just never imagine Mum having casual sex with some guy she met on holiday.'

'I could never really imagine your mum having sex at all,' Bram interrupted.

'Shut up and listen.' Mattie couldn't help smiling. It was true, of course. Mattie had never been able to imagine it either. Mary wouldn't even take her clothes off in front of her own daughter, let alone a man.

'Sorry, what were you going to say?'

'I was just going to say I was pleased she went off with someone she loved even if they did split up.'

'Yes,' Bram said. 'There's got to be a way of finding out exactly where she went.'

Mattie shrugged then leaned down and kissed him again. 'You're the ace detective. You tell me.'

Bram looked thoughtful. Then he sat up and grinned. 'I

know. What about doctor's records . . . they get passed on when you move around, don't they?'

Mattie shrugged. 'No idea.'

'What's the name of that doctor . . . the one who your mum went to?'

'Dr Kirkpatrick.'

She'd been brilliant. Getting Mum into the hospice . . . making sure Mattie was all right. Saying she would always be there if Mattie needed anything.

'She'll have them. They're bound to say what hospital Mary was in when she had you and stuff like that.'

She was infected by his enthusiasm. 'You're brilliant, Bram. You know that?'

He grinned. 'If I'm going to spend the rest of my life with you I want to know where you come from, don't I?'

'Are you?'

It wasn't like Bram to talk about that kind of thing. They were both far too young to think about lifetime commitments. There was so much to do first. That trip to Sri Lanka . . . she could afford it now.

'Am I what?' He rummaged in the bag and came up with an elastic band to tie back his hair. She noticed he didn't look at her.

'Thinking about spending the rest of your life with me?'

He finished messing about with his hair. 'Maybe,' he said. 'I mean you could be a changeling . . . a child swapped at birth. I'd like to know what I'm in for.' Bram was into all the fantasy stuff.

'You mean I might really be a princess?'

'No . . . I mean you might really be a goblin.'

She laughed as he leaned over to kiss her. Then she went red. Everyone must be watching. First tears and sobs, now kisses and laughter. Everyone would think they were on something. But she kissed him back just as hard. *Oh, Mum . . . if you could only see me now you'd have a fit.*

Eventually he let her go. 'Come on,' he grinned. 'You're getting me all steamed up.' He pulled on his jeans and trainers. He threw the towel at her. 'Let's go.' Bram could never sit still for five minutes.

'Where?'

'Home, of course.'

He was nuts. 'Bram, we've only just got here.'

'Oh.' He looked crestfallen. 'OK . . . we'll go back tomorrow. Mattie, I've only got a few days off and if we're going to get to the bottom of this . . .'

'OK,' she sighed. 'Tomorrow.'

Kelly

'Where's Mum?' Kelly poked her head round the door of her father's study. He was sitting at his desk writing out cheques. He looked at her over the top of his glasses.

'She's gone out on Goose.'

Kelly stuck out her bottom lip. 'Honestly, Dad, why didn't she wait for me? She knew I wanted to go with her.'

Robert Cole took off his glasses and put them on the desk. 'Come in a minute, Kelly. Let's have a chat.'

Kelly sighed. She hated it when Mum went off riding on her own. Especially now school had finished and she didn't have to restrict her riding to one grabbed hour in the evening before doing her rotten homework.

She went in and sat down with a sigh. Her father took her small hand into his own. She felt the roughness of his palm. The callouses where he'd spent all yesterday chopping wood for the winter. He always did it. Every year at the beginning of August he began chopping wood for the winter. Kelly had watched him from her window. He had been attacking the logs like a man possessed. 'It's therapeutic,' he'd said once when she asked him why he didn't buy logs already chopped up like other people.

Her father was looking down at her hand in his. 'Kelly, you know this is a bad time of year for your mum.'

'I know.' Kelly frowned and chewed the inside of her mouth. She tucked a lock of her long dark hair behind her ear. She hated this time of year too although she always tried not to show it. The first two weeks of the summer holiday were always hell. Mum going around with a tragic face like Lady Macbeth and Dad just as bad. She did understand, she really did. She knew what they were going through. But she had lived in the shadow of August for all of her thirteen years and sometimes she could scream. 'I'm sorry, Dad. I didn't mean to be horrible.' She took off her glasses and rubbed them on the knee of her jodhpurs.

Her dad passed his hand around his dark beard. In the field beyond the garden a combine harvester threw up a curtain of dust as it cut a swathe across the cornfield like some metallic monster. Kelly thought of all the little creatures it was probably churning up into its deadly jaws. She hated the thought of things being killed and couldn't even bring herself to squash a spider.

'Kelly, it's really been tough for you, hasn't it?'

Kelly leaned up and kissed her father's cheek. He smelt of his usual cologne and a faint hint of fried bacon where he'd treated Mum to breakfast in bed that morning. Having him off work for a couple of weeks was some consolation. At least she had someone to talk to while Mum was playing tragedy queen. Kelly felt guilty. She really shouldn't think like that. It wasn't jealousy. She didn't really know what it was. You couldn't really be jealous of a person who wasn't there, could you?

Mattie

6

Katherine was surprised to see Mattie and Bram back so soon.

'Are you all right?' She glanced at Mattie anxiously.

Mattie looked pale. There were dark circles beneath her eyes.

'Yes,' she said. 'I'm fine.' Liar, she thought, I feel terrible, gutted if you really must know.

Bram put his arm round her shoulders. 'No, she's not.'

'No,' said Katherine. 'I can see that.' She was getting lunch. 'Stay for something to eat and tell me all about Porthland,' she said. Then she frowned. 'You know I really wish I could remember why that name rang a bell.'

'It's only a little place,' said Mattie. She sat down at the table. 'I shouldn't think anything earth shattering ever happened there.'

Over quiche and salad they told her about Lilac Avenue and the mystery of Mary's sudden departure.

Katherine shook her head in disbelief.

'I don't know what to say, Mattie. But whatever happened to Mary . . . she must have had good reason to do what she did. She never did anything without thinking carefully first.'

'I know,' Mattie said.

Somehow that made it even worse. Mary's lies had been deliberate, not just some quick fib to satisfy a child's curiosity.

'It must have felt strange,' Katherine said drawing Mattie into the front room while Bram did the washing up. 'Being in the house where your mum was raised.'

Mattie sat down on the sofa and gazed into the empty fireplace. 'Yes, it was. When I found out my grandparents hadn't died when Mum said, I thought maybe I'd remember the house. That she'd taken me there as a kid.'

'And did you?' Katherine was staring at her with concern in her eyes. Eyes that looked just like Bram's in the pale afternoon light. Her sympathy triggered a wave of self-pity and Mattie swallowed hastily to stop herself from bursting into tears. She shook her head and cleared her throat noisily.

'No . . . not the house.'

'Mattie, I'm sorry . . .'

'Did she ever tell you anything about her life before you knew her?' Mattie asked.

'Not a thing.' Katherine got up and poured herself a gin and tonic. She waved the bottle at Mattie. Mattie shook her head. 'Sometimes,' Katherine continued, 'I thought she'd never *had* any other life before she came here.'

'We moved around a lot,' Mattie said. 'We've stayed here longer than anywhere.' Mattie remembered a long, curving row of tiny, drab terraced houses. A place where once you closed your doors you were exactly the same as anyone else. Then there was a big caravan in a park somewhere close to a river. Mattie loved it. It was like being on holiday fifty-two weeks a year.

'Yes. I did gather that from one or two things she mentioned in passing but she never talked about her young life. I never really thought anything of it. Your mum was a very private person, Mattie.'

'Yes.' Mattie stretched out her legs and put her hands behind her head. 'So private she lied to her own daughter about her date of birth and about who her father was.' She felt guilty about the bitterness that crept into her voice.

Katherine sat beside her and stared into her glass. 'She must have had her reasons . . . I mean, let's face it, not many kids are interested in their parents' young lives anyway. It's all ancient history to them.'

'They're interested in who their father was,' Mattie said flatly.

'Yes.' Katherine didn't seem to know what else to say.

But Mattie knew Katherine was right. She had never given Mary's past a thought until all this came up. A few questions about her dad. She had been satisfied with the answers and never questioned their validity. There was just the two of them, Mary, Mattie and some distant memory of a holiday love affair. Mattie had been too busy leading her own life to think much about Mum's.

Bram came in drying his hands on a towel. 'Fit, Mattie?'

'Yep.' Mattie rose. 'Thanks for the lunch, Katherine.'

'You two don't sit still for five minutes.' Katherine smiled. 'Where are you off to now for goodness' sake?'

'Bram's promised to help me sort out Mum's things.' Mattie felt her heart turn over. It had got to be the worst job ever, sorting through a dead person's stuff. Especially when that person happened to be your mother. It would seem a violation . . . as if you were prying into her secrets even though nothing was private any more once you were dead. 'We wondered if we might find some clues amongst Mum's papers,' she continued.

'Yes, you might,' Katherine said. 'Any idea what you're going to do with her clothes?' she added gently.

Mattie shrugged. She hadn't really given it a thought. 'There aren't that many,' she said. 'You know she wasn't one for dressing up much.'

Mattie suddenly remembered the time Mary had turned up at a parents' evening in an old pinafore dress and man's shirt with old brown sandals on her feet. Mattie could have died. She had run home and locked herself in her room. Later, when they'd made it up, Mary said she didn't like drawing attention to herself by wearing bright colours but Mattie noticed she took more care with her clothes after that.

'She had her own style,' Katherine said kindly.

'Yes,' Mattie said and couldn't help grinning. 'Old fashioned.'

'Well, I know the church need things for refugees,' said

Katherine. 'See how you feel when you've gone through them.'

'No, it's OK,' Mattie said quickly. 'I'll take them all down there. Mum would have liked that.'

Katherine gave her a hug before they left. Mattie hugged her back. 'What would I do without you?' she said.

Katherine smiled. 'You'd manage.'

Sinbad was waiting by the front door. A neighbour had been looking after him while Mattie was away. She scooped him up in her arms and laid her cheek against his fur.

'He's missing Mum,' she said. She put the cat down and unlocked the door. There was a pile of mail . . . mostly junk. One or two for Mary. Mattie sighed. That's another job she had to do. Let people know Mary was dead. Although, come to think of it, there wasn't really anyone to tell. Just the electricity board, the council, Mary's book club . . . no friends . . . no relations.

Mattie swallowed quickly. It was strange, going into the flat. She half expected Mum to be there; to hear the familiar sound of her footsteps in the bedroom as she cleaned and tidied every single day before going to work, even though most of the time it was spotless already.

Sinbad strolled into the kitchen, tail held high. Then he came out and wandered into the sitting room.

'He's still wondering where she is,' Bram said.

'Yes,' Mattie said miserably. 'I know.'

In Mary's room the curtains were drawn across the window. Mattie threw them back. Sunlight streamed across the bedspread. She opened the fanlight. 'It's really stuffy in here.'

The room was neat and tidy. Even before she left for the hospice Mary had given it a going over as best she could. It was quite unlike Mattie's room. *Her* room was a tip. Clothes all over the place, bed unmade, posters hung at crazy angles when Mary liked everything square and symmetrical, Mattie's drawings scattered around. Mary had freaked out about it all the time until she finally gave up and stopped going in there. 'It's my space,' Mattie had said. 'What you don't see, you won't worry about.'

Bram sat down on the bed. 'It doesn't seem right,' he said. He ran his hand over his jaw.

'What?' said Mattie.

'Turfing out her stuff.'

'I know.' Mattie sat beside him.

He put his hand on her knee. 'Shall we give it a miss?'

'No,' Mattie said determinedly. 'It's got to be done.'

'Do you want to look for that birth certificate first?'

But Mattie wanted to put *that* off as long as possible although she had no idea why. 'Let's do the clothes first.'

Bram went into the kitchen to get some black bin sacks. Mattie opened the wardrobe door. Mary's clothes, all browns, greys, and blacks, were hung neatly. All skirts together, all blouses, all jackets. Her half dozen pairs of shoes, still in their boxes, were stacked to one side. The shelves—hankies, tights, scarves, belts, gloves—all carefully folded.

'God, she was so tidy.' Bram came back, unrolled a bin bag and tore it off. 'It's unreal.'

'You're not kidding,' Mattie said.

They stripped the wardrobe, folded the clothes up and stacked them inside the bags. Strangely, Mattie felt no sadness, only a slight pang of guilt as if Mary might come in any minute and see what they were up to.

'Right,' Bram said when they had finished. 'That birth certificate.'

Mattie swallowed. She couldn't put it off any longer. 'I expect it's in her bureau,' she said. 'There's loads of papers in there.' She felt tired, drained. Her mind as well as her body. All she really wanted to do was curl up and disappear somewhere. Disintegrate like they did in the transporter aboard the Star Ship Enterprise, then reappear on the surface of some other world.

Bram was staring at her. 'You sure you want to?'

Mattie nodded. 'Let's get it over with.'

Mary's bureau was as orderly as everything else. Her pens and writing paper were stashed in one of the drawers with a bottle of ink and a sheet of blotting paper. Mary always wrote her letters by hand. Small, neat handwriting. Not a bit like Mattie's scrawl that looked as if spiders had walked across the page. There was a little-used cheque book and paying-in book. Mary had settled all her bills with cash and only used the bank when she had to. 'Once you're on their computer,' she said, 'they can find out all about you.' She had even wanted to be paid in cash but her company refused. She had been annoyed at having to have her wages paid into the bank like everyone else.

'The solicitor wants all these,' Mattie said, putting the bank books into a large envelope. '. . . and any outstanding bills.'

But there weren't any. Mary had settled up everything as if she had known the exact day she was going to die.

In another drawer they found Mattie's old school reports, her swimming certificates, her cycling proficiency diploma. Little mementos brought tears to Mattie's eyes and quick, fierce kisses from Bram to try to ease the pain.

'Look.' Mattie held up a ribbon she had worn on her ninth birthday. 'I remember because it was the year we moved here and the first time I'd ever had a party,' she said. There were cards too, from friends at her new school. 'I had no idea she kept them all,' Mattie said, wiping her eyes.

'You were all she had, Mattie.'

There were other things too. A badge saying 'The World's Best Mum'. A dried up rose bud that Mattie had been given at a local flower show. A man had taken a shine to her and picked one of his best blooms to pin on her coat. Mattie held it up with a frown.

'What's wrong?' Bram asked.

'I remember the man giving me this,' she said. 'Mum was really strange. She grabbed me and pulled me away from him. She was really angry that I'd let him pin this on my dress.'

'Perhaps she thought he was a child molester?'

Mattie shrugged. 'Maybe. Although she never liked me talking to anyone I didn't already know.'

'Come on, Mattie,' said Bram. 'You know how possessive she was.'

'Yes.' Mattie remembered too well.

'My mum keeps all this kind of stuff too,' Bram said. 'She's even got those little identity bands they put on your wrist when you're born. You know, so you don't get mixed up with someone's else's kid.' He made a circle with his thumb and forefinger. 'Mine's so tiny I can't believe it ever fitted me.'

Mattie sat back. 'Well, there's nothing like that here. Nothing from when I was a baby. I suppose she chucked out a lot of stuff each time we moved.' She looked at him mournfully. 'Perhaps I wasn't ever a baby at all.' She managed a wan smile.

Bram grinned. 'I bet you were a fantastic baby.'

'Then where's my birth certificate, for goodness' sake?' She was beginning to feel angry. 'She must have thrown it out, it's the only answer.'

'Come off it, Matt, she wouldn't have thrown something like that away, not on purpose.'

She sighed. 'Not on purpose, no.' She sniffed. 'That's probably it. It just got lost.'

They exchanged glances. Mattie knew exactly what Bram was thinking. Mary never lost anything . . . her obsessive tidiness saw to that. A place for everything and everything in its place, she always said.

She stuffed everything back into the drawer higgledy piggledy. She quickly thumbed through some more papers. It was really odd that Mum had kept so many things yet not the most important thing of all—the piece of paper that would tell her exactly when and where she had been born.

'It must be somewhere else,' Bram said suddenly.

'Like where?'

He shrugged. 'Maybe the solicitor's got it?'

Mattie bit the inside of her cheek. 'I can't think why she should have but I'll give her a ring just in case.'

Mrs Hodson was busy but her secretary promised Mattie she'd have a look then ring back.

The call came five minutes later. 'No, Mattie, sorry. Nothing like that at all.'

Mattie knew it was silly but she felt so disappointed she could have wept.

'You can get a copy,' Bram said, trying to comfort her. 'Some place in London. Mum'll know. Why don't you go and see Dr Kirkpatrick and have a word with her about Mary's medical records?'

'I'm sure that's confidential information or something,' Mattie said.

'I don't see it matters now she's dead.' He took both her hands. 'Go on, Mattie. She'll help you if she can. Give her a ring now, huh?'

Mattie shook her head. 'No, I'll go and see her.'

Mattie hadn't made an appointment so she had to wait until the end of surgery. She'd assured Bram she would be all right on her own. After all, she couldn't rely on him to be with her all the time. She sat in the waiting room reading a year old edition of *Country Life*. She thumbed through the glossy pages not really seeing anything. She didn't have a clue what she was going to say to the doctor. Can you look at Mum's records so I can find out when I was born? It sounded nutty. Maybe she would think up another reason for her visit? Or maybe she would just get up and walk out. No one would be any the wiser. Did it really matter anyway if her birthday wasn't the 19th August after all but some other day, some other month . . . or year. So what if she wasn't really seventeen. Who cared?

I do, Mattie thought miserably. I care. How can I have

gone through my life not being the age I thought I was. The thought was so mind blowing Mattie stood up quickly and threw the magazine impatiently back on the pile. Then one of the doors opened and Dr Kirkpatrick ushered out her last patient.

'Mattie!' She smiled at her then guided the old lady through into the reception. 'Wait there for your prescription, Mrs Day. The nurse will bring it out.'

'Mattie,' Dr Kirkpatrick said again. She held out her hand. 'Come in, come in.'

There was no escape now.

Mattie hated doctors' surgeries. They reminded her of the time she had sat in one with Mary, listening to the consultant droning on about terminal cancer. She eyed the couch with a shudder. The trolley, the instruments, lurking under the white cloth like an animal waiting for its prey.

In spite of all this, and for some reason Mattie could never work out, as soon as she sat down facing the doctor, everything suddenly came tumbling out. The visit to Lilac Avenue, the mystery of her mother leaving home with the man from the fair. How she changed her name from Hughes. She even told her about Amy Dray. The doctor steepled her fingers over her nose and listened intently. When Mattie mentioned Porthland she said a strange thing.

'Porthland?' she interrupted Mattie's flow. 'I've heard of that place.'

'That's what Bram's mum said too,' Mattie said, puzzled.

Dr Kirkpatrick shrugged. 'I'll think why in a minute. Go on, Mattie.'

When Mattie finished telling the story the doctor pressed a button on her intercom without comment. 'Have we still got Mattie's mother's records?' she asked.

The receptionist said they had.

'Could you bring them in, please.'

'Will they say the exact date of my birth?' Mattie asked anxiously.

'Possibly.'

71

'And where?'

'Yes, they should do.'

Mattie sat biting her nails. She had the sudden urge to tell the doctor something else. Disclosing the secrets of Mum's life had been easier than she'd thought. She imagined it must be like that to sit in a confessional and tell all your sins to the priest. Once you'd done it, it got easier and easier and in the end you found yourself telling him things you never meant to. Things that probably weren't sins at all. She wondered if the doctor would think she was having hallucinations if she told her about her people. The man, the woman, usually with huge, misty faces, leaning over her. Mattie wondered what she would think of Bram's ideas about childhood amnesia and his suggestion she visit a hypnotist.

She was just about to ask when the door opened and the receptionist came in.

'Thanks, Jackie.' The doctor took the bundle from her hand. Mattie had noticed her own notes were on the desk. A small folder compared to Mum's. Mattie had never been really sick. Just the usual childhood illnesses, chicken pox, rubella. Mary's envelope was bursting at the seams.

'Now,' Dr Kirkpatrick said. 'Let's have a look.' She pulled out a bundle and thumbed through. Hospital referrals, psychiatric reports, results of tests, scans, treatments, X-rays . . . She frowned then looked up at Mattie. 'No, Mattie, sorry. There's nothing before 1981 when you were up north. Do you remember that?'

Mattie shrugged. 'Vaguely, but we left when I was six or seven and went to live in the caravan.' She leaned forward. 'And Mum always told me I was *born* up north. Somewhere near Yorkshire. Maybe we lived there *before* 1981.'

'Yes.' The doctor turned over a card. 'After that you were with a Dr Ward in Kent.'

Mattie suddenly realized the enormity of what the doctor had said. She cleared her throat noisily. 'What, do you mean there's nothing before 1981?'

'That's exactly it. There's no medical history before 1981. It's not really surprising. Sometimes complete medical records don't get passed on when you move to another town. Although—' she broke off.

'What?' Mattie leaned forward.

Dr Kirkpatrick scratched her ear. 'Well, usually a summary card gets filled in with important details like dates of ante- and post-natal examinations, inoculations, things like that.'

Mattie knew what she was going to say. 'But there's nothing like that on Mum's.'

'No' Dr Kirkpatrick still looked puzzled. She thumbed through the pile of papers again. 'It almost gives the impression that your mum had never been registered with any doctor before then.'

'What about my records, then?'

The doctor picked up her folder. 'Your date of birth is on the front,' she said.

'But it's not my date of birth. It can't be.' She couldn't help sounding upset. Didn't the doctor understand what she was trying to say? 'I've told you about Mum's letter to her parents. It was written on the day I've always known as my birthday.'

'I'm sorry, Mattie. But we have no reason to disbelieve someone when they tell us their child's date of birth.'

'I realize that.' She didn't mean to sound so sharp. She had to keep calm. She didn't want to sound over-emotional. She swallowed quickly. 'Is there anything in my records about my birth?'

Dr Kirkpatrick looked through.

'No, there probably wouldn't be unless you'd been terribly premature or something. But there *should* be a record of your immunizations. They, at least, usually get passed on.' She frowned. 'I'm afraid they're not here. Nothing before 1981 either.'

'So before then I didn't exist?' Mattie's confusion was turning to anger.

73

'Yes, of course you did, Mattie,' the doctor soothed. 'I'm afraid these things do get mislaid sometimes.'

Mattie sat back in her chair. 'There's nothing about Mum's pregnancy at all then?'

The doctor shook her head. She was reading through some of Mary's old notes again. She frowned, quickly scanning a letter. 'That's odd.'

Mattie leaned forward again. 'What?'

'Your mum had problems with her periods, didn't she?'

'Yes.' Mattie remembered the days Mum went round with a hot water bottle held to her stomach, the days off work, the emergency rush to the chemist to get super-absorbent towels.

'Well, and this is before you lived here, but there was some talk of a hysterectomy. Your mum refused apparently.'

Mattie frowned. 'She never told me.'

'I guess she thought you were too young to understand. The doctor at that time put her on a course of tablets that helped sort her out for a while. At least, she never came for any more treatment.'

Mattie could no longer hide her impatience. 'But what's all that do do with me?'

'Well.' Dr Kirkpatrick waved a form at Mattie. 'According to this your mum was *nulli partus*.'

'Sorry?'

The doctor put down the paper. 'It means, Mattie, that at that time your mum had never been pregnant at all.'

Mattie drew her breath in sharply. She grew cold as if someone had flitted over her grave. 'That's daft. It must be a mistake.' She had a wild urge to laugh. Not only did she not know *when* she was born, or exactly where, it now seemed she had never been born at all.

Dr Kirkpatrick took off her glasses and laid them on the desk. She leaned forward. 'Mattie,' she said gently, 'has it ever occurred to you that Mary might have adopted you?'

Mattie stood up and paced the room angrily. 'No.' She

shook her head. 'She would have told me.' She sat down again and began fiddling with one of the studs on her jacket. A flush came to her cheeks. She stared at the doctor. I should stop all this now, she told herself. Stop it. Walk out. Just carry on like any normal orphan. 'Wouldn't she?' Mattie was almost shouting. 'Surely people tell their kids when they're adopted, don't they?'

The scene flashed again. Mum's pain-filled eyes . . . the bird-hand outstretched. '*Mattie . . . I want to tell you something . . .*' Why hadn't she waited until her mother could tell her what she wanted to say? Why did she go and get that stupid cup of tea? Was her whole life a mystery because she went to get a cup of tea. Mattie almost started laughing but clapped her hand over her mouth just in time. The doctor really would think she was hysterical . . . out of control.

'Not always,' the doctor was saying.

Mattie ran her hand through her hair. 'I can't believe she wouldn't have told me.'

'Perhaps she meant to . . . when you were eighteen.'

'Yes.' Mattie was beginning to calm down. It would explain the absence of the birth certificate . . . or would it?

'Surely there'd be papers, wouldn't there?'

'If it had all been done legally, yes, of course. And she would have had adoption papers and your birth certificate. Your solicitor may have them.'

'No, I've asked her.' Mattie drew a breath then continued. 'You said *legally*. Is it likely she might have got me *illegally*?'

Dr Kirkpatrick frowned. 'Well, there are ways and means if you've got the money.'

'I don't think Mum had any money.' Tears sprang to her eyes. She wiped them away angrily. 'It's just crazy . . .'

The doctor took her hand. 'Don't get upset, Mattie.' She squeezed Mattie's fingers then let go and began stuffing all the papers back into their folder. 'Look, you can apply to a place in London called St Catherine's House and they'll send you a copy of your certificate.'

'But surely you have to know your date and place of birth to do that.'

The doctor bit her lip. 'Yes. But look, Mattie, there's got to be a rational explanation for all of this.'

That's what Bram had said. But supposing there wasn't one. Supposing there was no *rational* explanation for any of it?

Then Mattie suddenly remembered something . . . someone else. The woman who owned the bookshop. *She* knew Mary well. Better than Mattie had realized. Maybe *she* would know something about Mary's past life that would shed some light on the mystery?

7

Mattie almost ran from the surgery. She hurried along the high street and up the narrow alleyway. The bookshop doorbell clanged as she went in.

The woman was sitting on a high stool writing out invoices. She looked at Mattie over the top of her glasses. Her face broke out into a wreath of smiles.

'Mattie! How are you?'

'I'm fine,' Mattie lied. 'Great.'

The woman climbed off the stool. 'How are you managing on your own, Mattie?'

'Fine,' Mattie said, not wanting to go into detail. 'I wanted to talk to you about my mum.'

The woman's eyes filled with bright moisture. 'Poor Mary. I do miss her little visits.'

Mattie fiddled with her thumbnail. 'Er . . . you said she talked to you about her past life.'

'That's right, she did.'

Mattie's hopes rose. 'I wondered if you knew anything about when I was a baby? You know, where I was born . . . stuff like that.'

The woman frowned. She took off her glasses and wiped them on the sleeve of her sweater. She looked puzzled. 'Surely you must know where you were born, Mattie?'

Mattie faked a grin. 'Yes, of course,' she fibbed. 'But I mean . . . I just wondered if Mum told you anything about the places we lived, stuff like that.'

The woman shook her head. 'Oh, no.' She laughed. 'We didn't talk about that kind of thing. It was much earlier than that. We were both away at boarding school you see and we'd both been bullied. You might say we swapped experiences. It made us feel better, knowing someone else had been as miserable as we were.' She laughed again. 'Your mum said she had never told anyone about it before. She said she'd felt weak and foolish allowing it to happen.'

'Oh, I see,' Mattie said, feeling sadder than ever. 'Poor Mum. She had a rotten time one way or another.'

'Yes. But I think you made up for it, Mattie. I'm sure she was very proud of you.'

'Yes.' Mattie didn't know what else to say.

'I was going to write a book about it and Mary was going to type up the manuscript for me.' The woman sighed and sniffed. 'But I've never got round to it and now it's too late for poor Mary to help me.'

'Yes,' Mattie said, crestfallen, hopes dashed again. She suddenly felt she had to get out. The last thing she wanted was the woman to start crying. 'Well, thanks,' she said hastily. She backed away, her hand on the doorknob. She felt the door being pushed from the other side and when she looked, someone was trying to get in. She stepped aside.

'What did you want to know for, Mattie?'

'Oh . . . nothing important,' Mattie fibbed again.

'Come and see me again, Mattie.' The woman put her glasses back on and looked hopefully at the customer.

'I will,' Mattie called, knowing she probably never would.

Mattie lay alone on her mother's bed. The room was bare. She had stripped the dressing table. Bundled everything into a box and shoved it into the empty wardrobe. Mary's hair brush, dressing table set, pale lipsticks that had been the only concession she had made to the wearing of make-up.

'I wish you'd let me stay,' Bram had said. He had been waiting when she got back. She had told him what Dr Kirkpatrick had said and about her abortive visit to the bookshop then asked him to go home. She needed time alone to think. She had kissed him goodbye, promising to meet him first thing.

She stood in the open doorway as he drove away. The wind shifted the hall lampshade and the light made dancing shadows on the walls. As she closed the door she saw her people at the end of the hall. They were receding as if they were running backwards away from her. Their figures were more shadowy, more fluid than ever before. Mattie had the sudden, scary feeling that this might be the last time she would ever see them. There was no doubt about it—each time they appeared they had become more and more indistinct—like a memory that fades with time.

'Maybe Bram's right,' she said to Sinbad later, curled beside her on the bed. 'They *are* people I really knew when I was little.' Although why they kept coming back to haunt her, she had no idea. She suddenly felt frightened. Was this to be the pattern of her life? People she relied on, people she loved, gradually fading away, melting before her eyes.

Mattie suddenly needed to talk to Bram more than anything in the world. She grabbed the phone beside the bed. She dialled his number. He answered sounding surprised and cautious. As if a phone call at this late hour might mean something awful had happened.

'It's only me,' Mattie said.

'Are you OK?'

'Yes . . . I just wanted to hear the sound of your voice.'

'That's a relief. What are you doing?'

'Just lying here thinking.'

'What about?' His voice changed tone as he made himself comfortable on the sofa.

'All kinds of stuff. What you said about my people . . . about them being part of my past.'

'They could be, you know, Mattie.'

'Yes,' she said. 'Maybe I could go to a seance or something. If I am psychic then a medium might be able to see them too . . . even talk to them.'

Bram sounded cautious. 'You don't want to get mixed

up in that kind of stuff, Mattie. That hypnotist might be a better idea.'

'I'm not sure I want anyone probing around in my subconscious.'

She heard Bram snort into the phone. 'You make it sound like an operation.'

'You know what I mean.'

'Well, it's up to you, Mattie. No one's going to force you to do anything you don't want.'

'Good.'

Down the phone, Bram stifled a yawn.

'Am I boring you?'

'No, sorry. I'm just knackered.'

'Why aren't you in bed then?'

'I was watching a movie.'

'Sorry I interrupted.'

'Don't worry. It was pretty corny.'

'I saw them tonight,' Mattie said. 'I think they're fading away.'

'Does that upset you?'

Mattie bit her lip. 'Kind of. I'm not sure really. I'd just like to know who they are before they disappear for ever.'

'Yes. You know I'll help you whatever you decide to do.'

'Thanks, Bram. I love you.'

'I love you, Mattie. I wish you hadn't made me come home.'

All of a sudden she needed him so much it was like a pain in the pit of her stomach. 'I'm sorry.'

'I can be there in seven and a half minutes.'

'Are you sure?'

'Are you kidding?'

She heard him slam down the phone.

Mattie put the phone down and got out of bed. She went to her own room. She opened her cupboard and drew out a large folder. There were lots of paintings and drawings inside. A Level Art work mostly; a folder full of sketches she had done just because she wanted to.

Tucked away at the back was a portrait of two people. Mattie's people. She put it on the floor and sat gazing at it. The two faces stared back at her through a haze of blue mist. Dark hair, dark hazel-brown eyes. The man, the woman. She'd had a job getting them right. But when at last she'd captured them exactly she half expected the mist to clear as if they had walked through it towards her. She thought they might suddenly cover their faces then take them away . . . peek-a-boo.

Mattie took the portraits back into Mary's room. She propped them up against the dressing table mirror. Then she got back into bed and lay staring at them until she heard Bram's key in the lock. She got up quickly and stuffed them into the drawer.

A few days later Mattie was woken by the phone shrilling in her ear. She stretched out her arm but the place next to her was empty. She could hear Bram whistling in the shower. She glanced at the clock and saw it was gone eleven. It took a moment to realize Mary wasn't here to tell her off for lazing around in bed.

'Mattie, is that you?'

It was Dr Kirkpatrick.

'Yes,' she said groggily.

The doctor was all efficiency. 'Mattie, I've managed to get in touch with the practice Mary's family were registered with in Porthland.'

Mattie was suddenly awake. She pushed back the duvet and sat up. Bram came in smelling of her peach shower gel.

'It's Doctor Kirkpatrick,' she mouthed in answer to his raised eyebrows.

He kissed her quickly. He was off with James on another antique-hunting trip to France. 'Got to go,' he whispered. 'See you Thursday.'

She touched his face then turned her attention back to the phone.

'What did they say?' Mattie found her heart was thumping painfully in her chest. She took a deep breath and swallowed hard. She had thought of nothing else for days. She hadn't done a thing at home. The flat was like a tip. The bin bags full of Mary's clothes were still on the bedroom floor. Washing up was piled in the sink.

'Miracle of miracles,' the doctor was saying. 'They found the Hughes's family records down in some dusty basement.'

'Great,' Mattie said, her heart in her mouth.

'Mary's are there up to 1978. Her parents' until they died. It looks as if no other doctor ever applied for your mother's records after she left home.'

Mattie bit the inside of her thumbnail. She could smell Bram's aftershave on her fingers. 'Oh.'

'You don't know where you lived between 1978 and 1981?'

'Up north, I suppose. But I told you, I don't know exactly where.'

Great, Mattie thought. No birthday, no mother, no Mattie and now three missing years.

'Mattie? Are you all right?'

'Yes, of course.' She pulled herself together. 'Thanks for finding out for me.'

'Mattie, if you want to try to find out about adoption you should go to Social Services.'

'Yes.' Mattie felt as if she was in a long dark tunnel. 'But Social Services where?'

'You could try Porthland.'

'Porthland?'

'Yes. Why not use that as a starting point, Mattie.'

'Right,' Mattie said although she couldn't really see what good that would do. Mary could hardly have adopted a child without her parents' knowledge. 'Anyway,' she said to the doctor, 'thanks for all your help.'

'I wish I could have done more.'

'No, that's great, thanks.'

'Let me know if I can be of any more help.'

'I will, thanks.'

Mattie put the phone down. Her mind whirled. Three years . . . three missing years. She racked her brains. Had Mum ever said exactly where they lived before they moved to Yorkshire? Mattie sighed and shook her head. She decided to take another look through Mary's papers. Maybe there'd be something there? Something they had missed.

Mattie ran into the dining room and threw open the lid of the bureau. On top, the flowers Bram had brought her the other day tipped over, spilling water into the inside.

Sorry, Mum, Mattie muttered. She ran into the kitchen and grabbed a tea cloth to mop it up. The antique bureau had been one of Mary's prized possessions.

Mattie thrust open drawer after drawer, spilling the contents, throwing them down as each one revealed nothing. Bills . . . all paid. Electricity, council tax, water . . . a few odd bits of correspondence. Nothing to tell Mattie about the missing years.

God, I'm going mad. Mattie ran her hands through her hair. She sat down on the carpet amongst the ruins of her mother's carefully organized paperwork. Sinbad came to rub himself against her bare legs. She picked him up and buried her face in his fur. He miaowed and struggled. The world might be ending but Sinbad hadn't had his breakfast.

Mattie rose and followed him into the kitchen. She opened a tin of cat food and spooned some into a saucer. There had got to be some way of finding out where they had lived. Where Mary had gone when she left Porthland with the man from the fair.

That's it . . . it came to Mattie in a flash. Of course, she had travelled around. She hadn't lived in one place at all for a while. Maybe Bram had been right. Things hadn't worked out with the fairground man. Mattie had never heard her mother say a good thing about a man in the whole of her life so perhaps he'd put her off the opposite sex for ever.

She had even been suspicious and shy of Bram's dad and never visited the house when he was there.

Mattie felt quite out of breath just thinking about it all. She figured Mary had left the fair and settled down somewhere in the north. Then she had adopted her. That would account for the missing years. Mary loved children, Amy Dray said so. She used to watch the children in the park for hours. Perhaps Mattie hadn't been a tiny baby. People adopted children of all ages. Maybe no one had known Mattie's real date of birth so Mary had chosen the first day of her new life. The day she had abandoned her life in Porthland and started over. She hadn't wanted her parents to trace her so she took a new name. A new name. A new baby. A new place to live. Mattie felt quite out of breath. But the doctor was right. She had got to have a starting point somewhere. And Porthland may as well be it.

Mattie almost shouted out loud. She felt like Professor Higgins. 'I've got it! By George, I've got it!' Full of new vigour, she phoned Katherine.

'I'm going back down to Porthland.'

'Oh, Mattie. Why?'

'Mrs Dray said the fair goes there every year. Maybe someone will remember Mum.'

'Mattie, it's years ago.'

'I know, Katherine, but I've got to try.'

'Will you go by train?'

'Yes. Please, will you tell Bram for me when he gets back.'

'Yes, of course. And take care, Mattie. Find somewhere decent to stay.'

'I will. I'll ring you when I get there.'

'Have you got enough money?'

The bank had released Mary's account. 'Yes,' said Mattie. 'Loads.'

She slammed down the phone and ran to put the things back into the bureau. She quickly tidied the papers into a pile and put all the mementos of her childhood back into their drawers. Opening up the small one at the bottom she noticed something. There was an envelope at the back. It had become wedged against the bottom of the drawer above. An envelope that had escaped the frenzy of her search. She released it and took it out. There was something bulky inside. Mattie felt it for a minute, like you do Christmas presents to try to guess what's inside before you rip off the paper. She couldn't make out what it was. She undid the flap of the envelope and opened it up. Inside was a small parcel of white tissue paper. Mattie unwrapped it carefully. Inside was a little child's expanding silver bracelet, still shiny and new as if it had never been worn.

'Oh.' Mattie held it in the palm of her hand. It was tiny but would have expanded to fit an older child's wrist. Mattie pulled a face. She couldn't ever remember having worn such a bracelet. But then she couldn't be expected to remember something that long ago. She folded it carefully back into its tissue paper and put it back into the drawer.

The only B & B with its 'vacancies' sign up was right in the centre of Porthland. The house's white-painted pebble dash made a perfect backdrop for the tubs of cascading scarlet geraniums and purple lobelia that stood outside the front door.

'I'll probably be staying a couple of nights,' Mattie said to the landlady. 'If that's OK.'

'You're lucky I've got a vacancy.' The woman led Mattie up the stairs to a cramped single room up under the eaves. 'It's only because someone cancelled. The town's always packed for the carnival.'

'Carnival?' Mattie dumped her rucksack down on the bed.

'You must know about the Porthland Sea Carnival?'

Mattie shook her head. 'No.'

'Oh, it's quite famous. It originated as thanksgiving for the survival of the fishermen but it's developed over the years into a full blown carnival . . . procession, fun-fair, firework display, the lot. It used to be held the third week in August but they changed the day some years back.'

'Sounds great,' Mattie said.

'It is. My husband's on the committee so he's out now getting things organized.'

'When is it, then?'

'On Saturday. You'll miss it if you go home Friday.'

Mattie smiled. 'Maybe I'll stay, then. I'll let you know.'

The room was tiny. There was hardly space to manoeuvre between the wardrobe and the bed. It was hot, stuffy and smelt of someone's stale cigarette smoke.

Mattie went to thrust open the window. The room overlooked the railway station. As she gazed out, a train arrived and disgorged a further horde of trippers before sounding its hooter and going back the way it had come. Beyond the station Mattie could see the bright, multicoloured roofs of the fun-fair rides and the waving green tops of the trees in the park. She unpacked quickly and went out.

There was a huge sign over the entrance. 'Saracen's Funfair.' A notice on the gate announced it opened at four o'clock. Mattie leaned her elbows on the top rail and gazed at the spread of silent rides and side-shows. It was a hot, humid afternoon and it seemed the fairground slept in preparation for a hectic night ahead.

Mattie glanced at her watch. An hour before opening time. She went to phone Katherine to tell her where she was staying then bought herself an ice-cream. She wandered along the sleepy high street, stopping now and then to gaze into the shop windows. Most were full of souvenirs. 'A present from Porthland', fluffy teddy bears with a ribbon saying 'Porthland' sewn into their ear. She found a second-hand bookshop tucked down a narrow alley between Woolworths and a charity shop. In there she found a dusty, hardback copy of *Lord of the Rings* and bought it for Bram.

When she came to the sign that pointed to the park she headed off in that direction without really knowing why. It seemed as if something was drawing her there, some urge she was powerless to resist.

Along a side street, a flat-bed trailer was being decorated with a blizzard of white paper flowers. 1st Porthland Guides, announced a banner. Two burly men were trying to tie it to the tailgate but the wind kept snatching it away. They grinned good-naturedly at Mattie as she went past as if she was an old friend.

The park was almost deserted. Everyone must be down on the beach. There were a few picnickers snatching shade beneath the trees. Even the ducks on the pond seemed affected by the heat and swam languidly around in circles, desultorily pecking at bloated bits of bread as if they really couldn't care less whether they ate them or not.

Mattie sat on the grass. She had the same peculiar feeling she'd felt before. Everything was just as she remembered. The pond. The trees. The picnic area. The statue of some forgotten hero in the middle of one of the flower beds. The only difference was that everything seemed much smaller. And there was something else. Mattie felt a sudden wave of sick, heavy sadness. Something had happened here. Something horrible. But however hard Mattie racked her brains she could not think what it might have been.

She lay back, hands clasped behind her head. There was one thing she was sure of. She had been here twice before. Once with Bram. But the other time . . . All she knew was that it was a memory from early childhood—a memory that for some reason or other had been buried in her mind. It was only coming here, seeing this place again, that made her remember. If she had never come to Porthland, she might never have thought of the place again. Mattie shivered. It was a really weird thought. All those memories buried deep inside you. As if you had lived another life. A life that you had forgotten about completely.

At ten past four Mattie went through the fun-fair gate.

There was hardly anyone about here either. The chair-o-plane whirled emptily and the switchback had only one passenger—a teenage boy trying desperately to suck an ice lolly and hang on to his rock-and-rolling motorbike at the same time.

'Five shots a pound. Come on darlin'.' The dark-haired youth behind the rifle range flung his enticements at Mattie as she wandered past. She didn't know where to begin. Who to ask . . . even what to say.

'I'd be hopeless,' she said to the youth with a grin.

'Come on, you don't know what you can do till you try.' The dark eyes twinkled. Mattie stared at him. Maybe Mum's fairground lover had looked like that? Almost black hair, tanned skin . . . a flirty twinkle in his eyes. Irresistible to a twenty-five-year-old spinster whose only experience of men was a domineering father.

'On your own, then?' the boy asked.

'Looks like it,' Mattie flung back.

'Where's your boyfriend?'

'I left him behind.'

Mattie found herself flirting back. Perhaps fairground travellers all had the same charm?

'On holiday are you?' He leaned against one of the posts supporting the stall. He had broad shoulders and long, easy limbs.

Mattie shook her head. 'I'm looking for someone.'

'Someone like me?'

Mattie laughed. 'No, actually I'm looking for myself.'

She could see he didn't know what she was on about. She wasn't surprised. Who would?

He frowned. 'You a student?'

'Yes.'

'Brainy, are you?'

'I wish,' Mattie said.

'Who you really looking for?' She could see his curiosity was aroused. Two teenage girls were waiting on the other side for a shot at the targets. The youth took their

88

money and handed them their rifles then turned back to Mattie.

Mattie took the photo of Mary as a young woman out of her bag. 'Her,' she said.

The boy gazed at it. 'Blimey, it was taken years ago.'

'Yes,' said Mattie flatly. She had thought it better to bring the picture of Mary as a young woman. 'I know.'

He handed it back to her. 'Never seen her before in my life,' he said. 'You'd best ask my old man. He's running the Hall of Mirrors today. He and my ma have been with the fair all their lives so they might remember her.'

'Thanks.' Mattie smiled. 'Maybe I'll come and have a go later after all.'

'I'll look forward to it.' He grinned lopsidedly.

Mattie looked at him from under her lashes. She liked this swarthy fairground boy. If it hadn't been for Bram she might . . .

The boy's dad was drinking something out of a grubby mug with Saracen's Superb Fun-fair printed round the side. He was an older version of his son.

'Excuse me.' Mattie's heart was in her mouth. She wasn't used to just going up to people boldly and asking odd questions. It was easy with someone your own age but she felt shy and awkward with older men. She always had. She supposed it came from being brought up without a dad.

The man took a last gulp of tea and threw the dregs on to the grass.

'Want to go in, love? It's only fifty pence.'

'Er . . . no,' Mattie said. 'I actually wanted to ask you something?'

'What's that?' He looked a bit suspicious.

She took a deep breath. In for a penny, in for a pound, she thought and plunged ahead. 'I wondered if you had ever known a woman called Mary Hughes?'

'Who wants to know?'

'Er . . . me. I'm a relative. I understand she joined the fair some years ago.' She handed him the picture. 'This is her.'

89

He stared at it with a frown on his face. 'How long ago was she supposed to have been here?'

'Seventeen years.'

It sounded daft. A lifetime. No one would remember someone from seventeen years ago.

The man pulled a face and shook his head. He went on gazing at the photo. 'Worked here, did she?' he asked.

'I'm not sure. She may have done.'

The man shrugged broad shoulders. He handed the photo back to Mattie. 'Don't remember her. Better ask the wife. She deals with hiring and firing.'

Mattie's heart sank. 'Oh, no . . . she wasn't exactly hired,' she began.

A woman with a horde of excited children trundled up with a pushchair.

'Where . . .?' Mattie began lamely.

'Over there.' He pointed an oil-stained finger. 'Madame Rosella.'

Madame Rosella's caravan was tucked away from the noise and whirl of the rides. The place was beginning to liven up as people drifted in from the beach. The air became inflated with music and lights. 'It's Now or Never' blared out from the switchback and a party of youngsters were trying to smash into one another on the bumper cars to the heavy drumbeat of Status Quo.

'One way round and no bumping,' the operator yelled over the tannoy. Mattie couldn't see the point if you weren't allowed to bump.

A small girl sat outside Madame Rosella's caravan. She was reading a teen magazine. There was a board propped up against her table. 'Madame Rosella—Fortunes told. Cards. Tea Leaves.' Then there was a list of famous people whose palms Madame Rosella had read.

'A pound,' the girl said as Mattie went up to her. She stared up at Mattie through a scruffy fringe of pale hair.

Mattie fumbled in the back pocket of her shorts and came up with a coin.

'Ta.' The girl inclined her head towards the door. 'Up them steps.'

'Thanks,' Mattie said.

It was semi dark inside. A navy curtain embroidered with the sun and moon hung across the middle of the room. The air smelt of stale tobacco smoke and a rumour of fried onions.

Madame Rosella sat in front of the curtain. She was reading *Woman's Own* by the light from the illuminated crystal ball in the centre of the table. She was short and plump, with a pale, puffy face and a halo of blonde hair. She looked up as Mattie came in. She narrowed her eyes. Mattie felt like a fly that had blundered into a spider's web.

Madame Rosella bundled the magazine underneath the table and went on staring at Mattie with a slight frown creasing one darkly pencilled eyebrow.

Then she seemed to come back to reality and indicated the seat opposite.

'Sit there, dear.'

'Thank you.'

Mattie sat down. She was sweating. She rubbed the palms of her hands on her shorts and sat fiddling with the strap of her bag. She crossed and uncrossed her ankles. 'I haven't actually come to have my fortune told,' she said quickly before she could chicken out and flee without saying a word.

Madame Rosella still looked puzzled. 'No, I can see that. What is it, dear? What's troubling you?'

Mattie drew her breath in sharply. There was something about Rosella's eyes . . . She appeared to be looking right into her brain. It seemed as if the woman could see all the terrors and turmoils of Mattie's past few days. Mattie took hold of herself. It was stupid, she told herself. Just because she's sitting in front of a crystal ball it doesn't mean she's really psychic. It's just an act . . . a way of making a bob or two.

To Mattie's surprise, Rosella reached under the table and

91

switched off the crystal ball. Then she rose and went to the door. 'Allie,' she yelled.

'What?' The urchin face appeared from round the corner.

'I'm not open, right.'

'But . . .'

'But nothing. Just skidaddle will you. Go and get a Coke or something.'

Rosella closed and locked the door. Then she drew back the curtains and opened the window. 'It's as stuffy as a vicar's kitchen in here,' she said. 'The customers expect it, I'm afraid.'

'Yes,' Mattie said lamely.

Then Madame Rosella sat back down opposite. She put her hand on to the table. 'Give me your hand, dear.'

Mattie hesitated.

'Oh, don't worry, I'm not going to tell you you're about to meet a tall dark stranger. I can see you're too intelligent for all that nonsense. I just want to hold your hand, that's all.'

Mattie put her hand out. Madame Rosella's flesh was cool, her skin rough and dry. The woman took a deep breath and closed her eyes. Then she opened them wide and went on staring closely at Mattie.

'What's your name, dear?'

Mattie told her.

She let go Mattie's hand and drew a packet of cigarettes from the sleeve of her voluminous blouse. She lit one and puffed out a smoke ring.

'I only do this fortune telling lark to make a bit of money,' she explained. She leaned forward and Mattie smelt the slight odour of perspiration mixed with eau de cologne. 'But I am a medium, Mattie. And I do like to help people to understand things that happen to them. People like you, Mattie. Do you know what I mean?' Her face was so close Mattie could see where her mascara had run into the lines beneath her eyes.

Mattie swallowed. She could hardly believe what she was hearing. She hadn't said anything to Rosella. And yet, Mattie had the uncanny feeling that the woman knew all about her. Any other time she might dismiss all this as a load of rubbish. But she heard a ring of real concern in Rosella's voice. A real desire to help. She had come to ask questions about her mother but she had the sudden, crazy feeling she was going to end up telling Rosella something she'd only ever told one other person in the world—Bram.

Kelly

Kelly's father was still staring at her, waiting for her to say something. Something that would reassure him that things hadn't been tough for her at all. That she'd learned to accept the fact that her parents' existence was overshadowed by something that really had nothing to do with her at all. Something that had happened three years before she was even born.

She shrugged, still feeling guilty. It was bad enough for them without her making things worse. 'It's been OK,' she said.

He sighed. 'Living with our sorrow when it really hasn't got anything to do with you can't have been easy, Kelly.' She heard his voice catch with something like anguish. She looked at him and saw the sorrow, the raw pain in his eyes.

Kelly felt helpless. 'You can't help it,' was all she could think of to say.

To her dismay, Dad's eyes filled with tears.

'Dad, I'm sorry. I'm really sorry.'

She flung out her arms but her father didn't seem to see them. He rose and went to gaze out of the window. In the distance Kelly's mum, Beverley, was cantering her chestnut along the wide verge of greensward beyond the half harvested cornfield. Her dark hair shone almost black in the sunlight. Goose slowed to a trot then horse and rider disappeared into the wood. Robert wiped his eyes and turned back to his daughter.

Kelly sat dumbly in the chair. What an insensitive twit she was. She really hated seeing her parents upset. She jumped up, ran to her father, and clasped her arms round his waist. 'I do understand, Dad. Honestly.'

'I know you do, pet.' Dad took his hanky out of the

pocket of his jeans and blew his nose. 'Look, are you sure you don't mind staying with Gran while we go off for a few days?'

It was strange but Dad never said the name of where they were going. They always just 'went off' for a few days. Kelly knew *where* they went, of course. It wasn't exactly a secret. It was just that neither Mum nor Dad could ever bring themselves to actually say the name.

'No, 'course not,' she reassured him. 'Mum's persuaded her to let me take Starlight. There's great bridle paths round the village and the local riding school's having a gymkhana apparently. Mum said I could enter.'

For one minute, her dad looked panic stricken. 'I don't want you riding off on your own, Kelly.'

She *almost* told him not to be paranoid but bit back the words. That kind of thing was just about the last thing you said to her dad, or her mum for that matter. The kind of thing that made them both throw a wobbly.

'I won't. There's that girl Laura down the road from Gran, remember?' She tried not to sound too impatient. 'She's got a pony. Gran's organized it so we ride out together.' Kelly made a little-girl face. 'Dad, it is OK, isn't it?'

Robert patted her shoulder. 'Yes, as long as you promise not to go out alone.'

'Dad, you really don't think Mum would let me go at all if she thought that, do you?' Kelly was never allowed to go anywhere on her own . . . ever.

He shook his head. 'No, 'course not.' He gave a deep sigh. 'Right, better get on with paying these bills before we go away. Your mum won't be long, Kelly. Be nice to her, huh?'

'I will, Dad.'

But when Kelly went out she noticed her father wasn't filling in any more cheques at all. He was sitting staring at the photograph of her sister, Sarah, that had sat on top of his desk for as long as Kelly could remember.

Mattie

8

'Well, I can tell you something.'

Mattie watched as Madame Rosella stubbed out her cigarette in a silver ashtray on the draining board. She had drawn back the dividing curtain to reveal a sparkling kitchen with living room and bedroom beyond, windowsills festooned with sprays of plastic flowers. 'They're not spirits.'

'How do you know?' Mattie breathed. She still felt stunned. Rosella hadn't laughed when she'd told her about her people. She had listened to every word she'd said, just nodding now and then with a look of sympathy on her face.

'Because I'd be able to see them if they were.'

'Ghosts, then?' Mattie said. She was almost ready to believe anything the woman told her.

Rosella shrugged. 'Same thing really. Restless spirits . . . ghosts. But ghosts are usually tied to the place where they died.'

'I've often wondered if I was . . .' Mattie hesitated. This was going to sound stupid. Like something out of a bad horror movie.

Madame Rosella leaned forward. 'You were what, dear?'

'Er . . . possessed in some way,' Mattie said. She had never voiced that fear before. Even to Bram. It seemed so crazy, like some gothic tale of damned and evil spirits. Even crazier now she'd actually said it.

Rosella took it in her stride. She leaned her chin on her hand and said, 'I don't think so, Mattie. I would have known straight away. You know, Mattie, I always knew I was psychic, right from when I was a kid. *My* imaginary friends were spirits of people that I saw all around. I've got a whole shelf of books on the subject but no one's ever come up with a good explanation as to why some people can *see* and some can't.'

'I suppose it's just a gift,' Mattie said.

'Yes. Not always a welcome one, I can tell you.'

'My boyfriend thinks they might be people in my memory . . . people I knew when I was little.'

'Yes, he could be right. If they are then I reckon you keep seeing them for a reason.'

'Like what?' Mattie asked.

Rosella stroked the soft layers of flesh at her neck. 'Something traumatic that happened . . . something that had a real effect on you when you were little. Something that you've consciously forgotten but it's still there, buried somewhere in your brain.'

'That's what Bram said too.'

'He's quite clever, this boyfriend of yours.'

'Yes.' Mattie felt herself blush. 'He is.'

'You know,' Rosella continued. 'There's a theory that ghosts are projections of unhappiness or desperation, left behind after violent or sudden death or great pain. People who had something important left to do and can't quite let go of their earthly life.'

'Yes, I've read about things like that.'

'And I just wonder if that's what's causing this couple to appear in front of you. Their unhappiness has left an impression on you that's never faded.'

'But they're *not* unhappy. They're always smiling, and anyway you said they weren't the spirits or ghosts of dead people.'

'That's right. And this is what I can't work out.'

Madame Rosella ran her hands thoughtfully over the crystal ball in front of her. Then she looked up at Mattie. 'Mattie, I think the projections could be coming from your unhappiness as well as theirs.'

'But if something *that* terrible happened and it had to do with me, surely I'd remember?'

Rosella shook her head. 'Not necessarily. The brain has a way of shutting terrible things out. It's sometimes the only way we survive. Haven't you read those dreadful stories of people who were molested as children . . . sometimes their minds have shut it out completely.'

'Yes,' said Mattie. 'I know.'

'Have you thought of going to see a hypnotist, dear?'

'My boyfriend thought it might be a good idea,' Mattie said. 'But I've read about therapists putting ideas into your head. Making you believe things that never really happened to you at all.'

Madame Rosella shook her head. 'That shouldn't happen. Not if you go to a proper hypnotherapist. Someone who'll just listen to you and not put ideas into your head by talking to you when you're under . . .'

'That's what scares me,' Mattie said. 'Being *under*, not knowing what you're saying.'

'You *will* know,' Rosella said. 'You'll only forget if the hypnotherapist tells you to forget.'

'It still scares me.'

'You might find out something about yourself you'd really rather not know.' Rosella looked at her shrewdly. 'Is that it?'

'But I *do want* to know. More than anything.'

'Well, then I think that's what you should do. They can take you right back to your infancy, you know. I knew someone once who had a phobia about being strangled. It turned out their umbilical cord was round their neck when they were born. Now . . .' Rosella glanced at her watch. 'I'm sorry, I really had better open up. Is that why you came? To ask me about these visions of yours?'

'No.' Mattie told her swiftly the real reason for her visit. She took the picture from her bag and showed her.

'No, sorry, dear.' Rosella glanced at it then handed it back. 'Don't remember her at all and I've got a good memory for faces.' She stared at it for a moment longer then handed it back. 'Sorry, dear.' Then, seeing Mattie's disappointment she continued, 'Look, I'll ask around. Come back tomorrow, maybe someone *will* remember.'

'Can I leave it with you, then?' Mattie put the photograph on the table.

'If you like. I'll show it round later. See if anyone can remember her.'

'Thanks, Rosella,' Mattie said gratefully.

'And you go and see that hypnotist. Those people of yours, I've got a feeling they might be going through the same thing as you.'

Mattie got up and hitched her bag on her shoulder. 'What do you mean?'

'Well, if you're seeing them . . . maybe they're seeing you.'

Now that was something she hadn't thought of.

That night, Mattie tossed and turned, unable to sleep. Music from the fun-fair stole through her open window. It sounded ghostly, as if it was coming from another dimension. Then, soon after midnight, everything went quiet. She missed Bram dreadfully. She put her arms round the pillow and eventually drifted off to sleep with her cheek sweating against the horrible nylon pillow slip that snagged at her fingernails every time she clutched it.

Then it was morning. A shaft of sunlight angled itself across the narrow bed. It caught the blue-black highlights in Mattie's hair. She opened her eyes to take hold of the new day, surprised and unaware she had even slept. She felt better, a new sense of purpose. She thrust back the covers. Today she would get in touch with Social Services like Dr Kirkpatrick had suggested *and* she might find that hypnotist. There was bound to be one in Yellow Pages.

She asked the landlady if she had a copy.

'In the drawer in the telephone table,' the woman told her.

Mattie skipped breakfast. She thumbed through the

directory. Hypnotherapists. She was surprised to see there were four in the town. She chose one with lots of letters after his name. He was attached to a health clinic where you could be treated for all kinds of things. She didn't want to surrender herself to some quack.

A woman answered the phone. 'I'll just have a look in the book,' she said in answer to Mattie's request. Mattie heard the sound of pages being turned. The woman came back. 'Three o'clock this afternoon all right?'

'Great,' said Mattie. 'Thanks.'

Then she called Social Services. It was unlikely Mary had adopted her here in Porthland but it was worth a try. She had woken with the determination not to leave any stone unturned . . . or turn unstoned as Bram would say. Bram. Her heart skipped. She wished she didn't miss him so much. It scared her . . . The thought of not being able to go anywhere, do anything, without missing him. She hadn't wanted that. Now Mum had gone she'd wanted to be free.

She dialled Social Services' number with a sigh. If she got this sorted, then she'd have time to think about her future. But for some reason she couldn't explain, she felt she had no future. After all, how can you have a future if you don't even exist?

Mattie bit the side of her thumbnail, waiting for someone to answer the phone.

At last, someone did and Mattie began again.

'I'm sorry,' the man said, 'we can't give out information to just anyone.'

'But I'm—'

'Sorry,' he said, unyielding. 'You must appreciate we have to be very careful.'

'Yes,' Mattie agreed reluctantly.

'Look,' he said more kindly. 'What you have to do is apply to the Registrar General.'

'Oh, where's he, then?'

The man gave Mattie an address in Lancashire. She scribbled it down on the back of the Yellow Pages.

'You write to them and they'll send you a form. You fill in all your details and they'll take it from there.'

But I don't *have* any details, you stupid man. Mattie felt like shouting down the phone. A false date of birth. Somewhere up north. Mary Browne or Mary Hughes. It would be like looking for a needle in a haystack.

Mattie slammed down the phone.

'Thanks for nothing,' she muttered. Then thought that was the first sign of going nuts—talking to yourself. It was probably too late. She already was.

She tore off the corner of the directory where she had written down the address and stuffed it into her bag.

The phone rang as she turned to go. The landlady appeared from the kitchen, drying her hands on her apron.

'Sorry,' Mattie said although she didn't know why.

Outside, the early morning sun had broken its promise. It was pouring. The geraniums were weeping raindrops on to the red polished doorstep and, on the roof, seagulls had arrived to take sanctuary from a mutinous sea. They squawked derisively at Mattie as she turned up her collar against the rain and headed towards town.

It was hours until three o'clock.

She found a café along the seafront. The bell clanged as she went in. One or two bedraggled holidaymakers looked up from their eggs and bacon. Mattie bought a cup of coffee and a doughnut and sat down by the window staring out at the grey ocean.

The tide was in and great waves hit the sea wall sending explosions of white foam high up into the air. The noise was like the distant boom of cannon fire. Mattie wondered about the carnival float. If the snowstorm of paper flowers would fall to bits in the rain. If all that hard work would have been for nothing.

She leaned her chin on her hands. She felt full of apprehension. What did a hypnotist do? Did he swing a pendulum in front of you until you fell asleep and yielded the secrets of your mind? Or was that stuff just invented by the movie makers? She had meant it when she told Bram she didn't fancy anyone probing her subconscious.

But that had been before Rosella. It was different now. Rosella actually knew people who had discovered things about themselves. Things they hadn't even known existed.

The clinic was in a tiny back street set behind the terrace of small shops that flanked the promenade. A policeman had pointed Mattie in the right direction.

'You look a bit wet, love,' he said.

She hadn't even noticed.

Mattie's fingers hovered over the bell. Charles Amery, M.A.E.P.H., R.M.N., DIP.HYP. it said on the brass plaque. She couldn't begin to guess what all the letters stood for. Dip. Hyp. sounded like a dance, something like hip-hop, or be-bop. She began to giggle then clapped her hand over her mouth. They would be coming to take her away if she did-n't watch out. She felt a sudden urge to run anyway and got half-way down the steps before she pulled herself together and went to press the bell not once, but twice just to make sure someone heard. The sound of it clamouring down the inside hallway seemed to set a seal on her deter-mination.

She had been back at the B & B for an hour when there was a knock at her door. She almost jumped out of her skin.

'Are you in there, dear?'

Mattie came to. 'Yes.' She was still in a daze. The hyp-notherapist's words whirlpooling in her brain, round and round, until she thought she was going to freak out.

'There's someone downstairs to see you.' The landlady's voice came from outside the door.

'Me?'

'Yes, dear.'

'Oh . . .?' Who on earth . . .? Mattie rose to open the door.

'Who is it?'

'Me,' a voice said from half-way up.

The landlady stepped aside just in time as Mattie flew out on to the landing. She clung to Bram, almost making him lose his balance at the top of the stairs. 'Hey . . .' he hugged her back. She felt the tension ease out of her.

'This is only a single room,' the woman said primly. 'There's not enough room for two.'

'It's OK,' Bram said quickly.

Mattie dragged him inside. 'What are you doing here, Bram?' She kissed him hard then plonked down on the bed and patted the place beside her.

'I've got something to tell you, Mattie.'

She hardly noticed his troubled face.

'And, boy, have I got something to tell you.' She could hardly get it out quick enough. 'Hey, you're soaked.'

'I had to park miles away, the place is packed.'

'I know,' she said. 'It's always the same in August apparently.'

She pulled off his damp coat and hung it on a hook behind the door. Then she sat back down. 'Bram, I'm so glad you're here.'

'Me too,' he said flatly. He took both her hands in his. 'Mattie . . . I—'

She held a finger to his lips. 'Let me tell first, please.' She felt ready to burst.

He stared at her eager face. 'OK,' he said without smiling.

She took a deep breath. 'Well, I've been to see a hypnotherapist. He was absolutely brilliant. Rosella told me—'

'Who?'

She laughed. 'Oh, Bram, I forgot. OK, I'll start at the beginning.'

Bram sat with his hands between his knees, his head

bowed. He looked as if he had a great weight sitting on his shoulders.

'. . . and so I found Mr Amery in the Yellow Pages and toddled along to see him this afternoon.'

'What did he say, Mattie?' Bram didn't look at her. It seemed as if he couldn't meet her eyes.

She got up and went to gaze out of the window. It had stopped raining at last. The sun sparkled on the laundered rooftops catching silver in the slate tiles and turning them to mirrors. A couple of gulls rose from a chimney stack and headed off towards the sea.

'Mattie!' Bram was losing patience. 'What did he say?'

She turned and leaned her backside against the windowsill. Her eyes shone. 'Bram, it was really weird. He took me right back to when I was really young. You know, I was petrified at first but it was really easy. I hardly even knew he was doing it.'

'How did he?' Bram asked.

Mattie raised her clenched fist then held up one finger at a time. 'He did it year by year . . . each time he raised a finger I found myself remembering stuff from when I was a kid.'

'And . . .?' Bram ran his hand over his jaw. He glanced at her then shifted his gaze to one side.

'Well, I remembered everything.' She was having a job to calm her heart's wild beat. It had been the same ever since she left the clinic and walked in a daze back to the boarding house. She could hardly even remember coming up to her room and sitting on the bed, gazing at herself in the mirror for almost an hour before Bram turned up.

'What kind of thing, Mattie?'

'Being here, Bram,' she said breathlessly. 'I remembered the park and the beach and the carnival.'

'The carnival?'

'Yes. The Porthland Sea Carnival. Have you heard about it before?'

'Yes,' he said. 'I know all about it.'

Mattie frowned slightly. How come Bram knew about the carnival when he'd never even heard of Porthland before Mary died?

'Anyway . . .' She shook off a creeping feeling of unease that was beginning to invade her mind. She was so anxious to tell him what had happened that her bewilderment at his words slipped away before she even had time to think about it. 'I described the floats and the flowers, colours, people . . .' She came back to him and sat down, one leg curled beneath her body. 'And the music,' her eyes shone as if she was there again hearing the brass band. 'I'd got a windmill and it was red and green. I was sitting in a pushchair. I couldn't see the people I was with because they were behind me, holding on to the handle. Bram, I remembered it all!'

'Mattie . . .'

'Bram, I think it must have been Mum and her boyfriend pushing the pram. They must have brought me to see the carnival.'

'What makes you think that, Mattie?' Bram's tone was beginning to irritate her. Did he think she was making it all up?

'Because it *must* have been. I've been thinking about it. I bet she brought me here to see my grandparents. I mean, she did name me after her mother so she must have loved her, mustn't she? You don't call your kid after someone you hate, do you? Maybe they refused to make it up. You know, coming back with a fairground man and a baby as well. They probably just couldn't cope with it. Especially as they'd told everyone she'd gone to live with an aunt.' She grasped his hand. 'Bram, I don't care if I *am* adopted. It's just enough to know that Mum loved me and . . .' She knew she was rattling on but she was so excited, so relieved, she couldn't hold it all back. In fact she was so elated she had almost forgotten that she had begun to cry bitterly for no apparent reason just as the hypnotist felt she had been under long enough and had brought her back to

108

the present with the prearranged signal. She suddenly realized there really was something wrong with Bram.
Something horribly wrong. He was looking at her with
something like pity in his eyes. She had never seen him
look like that before.

She frowned, stopping suddenly her flow of excited
chatter. 'Bram . . . what's the matter?'

His eyes slid away. 'Nothing. What about your people,
Mattie? Isn't that what you wanted to find out about from
this guy?'

'I'm getting to that,' she said. 'Later, after the carnival, I
remembered being taken to the park. You see, I *knew* I'd
been there before. I described the gates and the pond. I
remembered lying under the trees with sun filtering
through. I was tired and happy . . . And then I saw them,
Bram. I saw my people.'

Mattie felt her eyes prick and fill. Hot tears fled down
her cheeks. She was crying again, just as she had cried in the
clinic only this time it was obvious why. They were tears of
relief, as if a whole burden of doubt had been lifted from
her shoulders.

'Mattie!' Bram put his arms round her but she pulled
back and reached for a tissue. She blew her nose loudly. He
was still gazing at her now with an ocean of sympathy in
his eyes. He let his hand rest on her knee.

She managed a grin. 'Sorry,' she said. 'I don't know why
I'm crying, this should be the best day of my life.'

She swallowed hard. 'Mr Amery thinks they're just two
people who came up to me when I was in my buggy,' she
went on. 'He reckons I was probably asleep and they bent
over me and woke me up. People often do that to little kids,
don't they? Frighten them when they really mean to make
them smile.'

'Yes,' Bram said flatly.

'He doesn't know why they made such an impression on
me. He said often things stick in our mind for no reason at
all, then something will trigger that memory off. He said I

109

could have been frightened, or I could have laughed at them. He said it doesn't matter really. The important thing is that subconsciously I've never forgotten them.' She drew a deep breath. 'Bram, I should have gone to see someone like him ages ago. All those years of thinking I was haunted or possessed or something.'

She hugged him impulsively. 'I still don't know why Mum lied to me, you know, about my date of birth and when my grandparents died. But I know she must have had a good reason, Bram. I—'

Mattie broke off. She couldn't ignore Bram's expression any longer. She realized suddenly what it was she could see in his eyes. It *was* pity.

She suddenly went cold. 'Bram?'

She suddenly felt terror invade her heart. Something dreadful had happened and she had been too blind, too full of her own selfishness to give him a chance to tell her. She felt her heart give its mad beat of panic. She shook his arm. 'Bram. What's wrong?'

'Mattie . . .' His voice broke and she saw to her horror that he had tears in his eyes. He put out his hand to stroke her face gently. He pushed back the long fringe of hair that had caught in her eyelashes. She had been so excited she hadn't even bothered to flick it back. He played with her fingers as if they were the most fascinating things in the world. Then he swallowed noisily. 'Mattie, you say your mum must have had a good reason to lie to you.'

'Yes,' she whispered.

'Well, you're right, Mattie,' Bram said huskily. 'She did.'

Kelly

Kelly shut the study door quietly although she didn't think her father would have heard it if she had slammed it with all her might.

Kelly went up to her room to wait for her mum to come back. Maybe she'd fancy another ride out later if she was feeling better?

Kelly threw herself down on the unmade bed. The room was a mess. Books, tapes all over the place. There were a couple of empty Coke cans on the windowsill. Her cat, Camel, was asleep on a pile of dirty washing in the corner. Kelly scooped him up and sat in a pool of sunlight that streamed across the bed. He hardly opened his eyes. She held him in her lap and stroked his pale, caramel-coloured fur until he purred with pleasure.

Then, restless and dying for something to do, she tipped him off. She didn't really know why but she went along to her parents' room, ducking low to avoid the massive oak beam that separated the two parts of the old cottage.

The bedroom door was open. Kelly tiptoed to the window and looked out. Dad was outside hosing down the Volvo. He'd only got it that week so she couldn't think why it needed cleaning. Its metallic blue paintwork was spotless and shiny. She heard the clatter of hooves and Goose trotted into the yard. She saw Dad go over and hold his bridle while Mum dismounted. They exchanged a few words then her father put his arms round Mum and they stood there for a minute, so close you could almost think they were one person. Kelly turned away, embarrassed. She always squirmed when her mum and dad did stuff like that.

She went to her mum's wardrobe and opened the door. She stood on tiptoe and felt beneath a couple of boxes. She screwed up her face with the effort as her fingers sought what they were looking for.

At last they closed over it and she drew it out. It was a photograph album, the fake leather cover well-worn and faded with years of handling.

Kelly sat on the bed and held the album in her lap. It had been ages since she looked at it. She wondered what Mum would say if she knew how she sneaked into her room from time to time and stole a look at it. She didn't even know why her mum had to hide it away . . . there were plenty of photographs all over the house. What was so special about these?

Kelly turned to the first page. Sarah as a new-born baby. Sarah in the bath, in the pram, at the christening, in the cot, in Gran's arms, under the Christmas tree looking like a little Scottish gnome in red tights and a red, plaid frock. Sarah lit from behind so she looked like a cherub. One of Dad's specialities. Sarah in the garden, Sarah with Mum, Sarah with Dad, Sarah looking just like Kelly at the same age, Sarah in the paddling pool, Sarah on holiday. Sarah laughing on the beach . . .

Sarah, Sarah, Sarah.

Kelly closed the album with a bang. She ran to the wardrobe and stuffed it back in. She didn't know why she was crying.

Her mother found her curled up on her bed, her soggy hanky stuffed in her mouth. Her face was red and blotched with tears.

'Kelly . . . sweetheart.' Kelly felt her mother rub her back the way she always did when she was upset or felt sick or woke in the night desperate to free herself from the recurring nightmare that had haunted her sleep ever since she learned the truth about her sister. 'I'm sorry I went off without you, I didn't realize you'd be so upset.'

Kelly reached out for her glasses and pulled them on. She shoved her hair back impatiently. 'I'm all right.' She could tell her mother had been weeping too. There were dark circles under her eyes. Eyes that seemed to look right through Kelly and on to search for someone in a distant landscape.

Her mum picked her hairbrush off the floor. 'Here, turn around, let me do it for you.'

She did as her mother asked, glad to be able to turn her back so Mum couldn't see her face. It was bad enough *them* going round with faces like a funeral, let alone her as well.

Her mother brushed the tangles out gently then took one of Kelly's scrunches and tied her hair back with it. She turned her daughter to face her. 'There, that looks great.' She pulled a face. 'Kelly, I'm really sorry. I just wanted to be alone for a little while.'

Kelly sniffed. 'Did you think you saw her, then?' Her mother had told her that she sometimes *saw* Sarah . . . as if she was a ghost or a spirit, so real she felt she could touch her, yet when she tried, the image always faded away. The thought of it made Kelly shudder and she wondered sometimes if Mum was off her head. Not that she'd be surprised. What had happened to Sarah was enough to make anyone go off their head.

Anyway, it wasn't that she *really* cared about Mum riding off on her own. They could go any time. But she couldn't tell her what had really upset her. It was stupid anyway. Crying for someone you'd never met.

'No.' Mum smiled gently then she dropped her gaze. 'I know you think I imagine it, but I do see her, Kelly . . .'

'I believe you, Mum.' She dragged out the words. 'And don't take any notice of me, I'm just being a twit.'

Mum hugged her. 'You're never a twit.' She smelt of horses and Chanel Number 5. Only Kelly's mum would have that combination. She giggled suddenly. It was OK, now. Mum's hugs always made it OK. She wished they could have made it OK for Sarah, too.

Beverley's face cleared. 'What's funny?'

'Your smell,' said Kelly.

Her mother managed a smile. 'Thanks very much.'

'You know, Goose and posh perfume, they don't really mix, Mum.'

Suddenly everything seemed all right again. They would make their annual pilgrimage. Cry for a couple of days and nights. They would go on somewhere else and by the time they got back home everything would be all right again.

Or at least, as all right as it would ever be.

Mattie

9

'It's all rubbish,' Mattie's eyes flashed angrily. 'None of that's anything to do with me. It's just coincidence.' She was walking to and fro in the tiny boarding house bedroom. Bram really couldn't have had any inkling how much such a crazy idea would upset her.

Bram was still sitting on the bed watching her pace up and down. 'It could be just coincidence, Mattie, but surely you want to find out?'

'No,' Mattie wrung her hands together. 'No, I don't want to do anything of the sort.'

She felt a deadly kind of misery creep over her. How could they say such a thing about Mary? How could they? She imagined them all talking about her, discussing it. The doctor and Katherine and Bram . . . all deciding what to do. She imagined the doctor saying 'she's got to be told,' and Bram volunteering to do the dirty deed.

Anyway, it was crazy, mad . . . such a possibility had never entered her mind. It was all some great conspiracy. Mary had always said that. Life was just one great conspiracy to try to drag you down.

'Mattie, you don't really mean you don't want to find out!' He flung out his arm to stop her walking past. He grabbed her hand but she wrenched it away.

'Don't tell me what I mean and what I don't mean,' she stormed. 'Leave me alone, Bram. Go back home. I don't want you here.' Her nostrils flared.

She didn't know why she lied. All she knew was that she couldn't stand the hurt in his eyes. Suddenly she had to get away. She grabbed her jacket and bag and flung herself out of the room. The landlady's head popped round the kitchen door as Mattie's boots clattered down the stairs.

'Is anything wrong, dear?'

'Get lost,' Mattie muttered.

'Mattie!' She was out of the front door before he caught her up.

He linked his arm through hers and made her slow down. It was no good anyway, she couldn't outrun him. She never had been able to. Even when they were kids. 'Come on,' he insisted. 'Let's walk.'

They strode along in silence. She began to feel better. She breathed in great lungfuls of sea air as if it would give her life. Bram's face was grim as he walked beside her. His long legs matched her angry strides with ease. She held her face up to the sea wind and felt it begin to clear the turmoil of her mind.

'Fancy a Coke?'

It was the first thing he'd said since they ran out of the boarding house.

She looked at him and pressed her lips together. She struggled against the impulse to fling her arms round him and apologize. She hated quarrelling with Bram but she'd had enough of saying sorry. So instead she just shrugged and said indifferently, 'If you like.'

The café was one of those American Diner types. Hamburgers and fries. Kentucky ice cream with cookie dough. The thought made Mattie want to throw up.

They sat opposite one another in a booth in the corner.

'Hi.' The waitress wore a bright smile and a fake American accent. 'What can I get you folks?'

'Just a couple of Cokes,' Bram said.

She wrote it down and tore off the top page of her pad. She stuck it between the pepper and salt and trotted off.

She came back minutes later with the drinks. 'Let me know if you guys want anything to eat.'

Bram smiled up at her. 'Thanks.'

Mattie sucked her Coke through the straw and gazed out of the window. She couldn't look Bram in the eye. If she did, she knew she would break down.

His hand slid towards hers across the table. 'Mattie, we've got to talk about this.'

She breathed heavily through her nostrils and chewed on the inside of her thumbnail. 'I said it's crazy, Bram. I don't want to talk about it.'

'At least let me tell you what Doctor Kirkpatrick said.'

She glared at him. Then, seeing the desperation in his eyes, she gave in. 'OK,' she said. 'But it's really nothing to do with me.'

She saw the muscles of his jaw tighten. He fiddled with his straw then looked back at Mattie. 'She said she was talking to one of the other doctors about Porthland,' he began, 'and he remembered what had happened there. *Why* it had rung a bell when you spoke about it to her.'

'I told you it's nothing to do with me,' Mattie insisted.

Bram sat back. 'OK, but at least let's discuss it, Mattie.' He was running out of patience.

'OK,' she conceded, not looking at him. She had bitten through her straw. She wrenched it from the glass, screwed it up and flung it into the ashtray. 'Go on.'

'The other doc remembered that a child had been kidnapped on the day of the carnival,' Bram continued. 'He couldn't remember the exact details but what he *did* remember was this.' He reached inside his leather jacket and drew out a folded piece of paper.

'Shall I read it to you?' he said cautiously.

Mattie shrugged. It was as if a barrier had come up between them. She *knew* Bram cared for her, *loved* her and would never do anything to hurt her. So why was she behaving like this? Why was she behaving as if she thought he was trying to trap her into believing something that wasn't true? She was getting as neurotic as her mum.

'If you want,' she said stiffly.

'It's a description of the kidnapped child that was circulated to all doctor's practices,' Bram explained. 'They were told to look out for . . .' He read from the piece of paper. '. . . a baby of twelve months with dark hair, deep brown

119

eyes and an olive skin. She was wearing a yellow Mothercare T-shirt and red shorts with a little white hat, brown sandals, and red socks. She was in a grey Mothercare pushchair with a bag attached to the handles that carried spare nappies, baby food, and her toys—'

Mattie put her hands over her ears. 'OK, Bram. That's enough.'

He leaned forward again. 'Mattie, you know it could have been you. It really could have been. Doctor Kirkpatrick tried to phone you, then called Mum when you weren't there. Mum remembered it then, too. It was in all the papers for weeks and weeks. Mattie, they even changed the day of the Carnival because it brought back too many bad memories for the town.'

It's funny, Mattie battled with the thought, how of all the reasons I've tried to imagine that Mum had for lying to me . . . I never ever thought that this might be it.

She felt her throat close up. 'You can't honestly think Mum would have done a thing like that,' she said furiously. 'Not taken a baby away from its parents.' She shook her head. 'You've got to be some kind of a nutter to do that.'

She loved children. She used to sit in the park and watch them for hours. Amy Dray's words hurled themselves into Mattie's mind.

'OK, then, Mattie,' Bram was saying. 'You tell me where she got you. She'd never been pregnant. Mum said it was very hard for a lone parent to adopt a kid in those days.'

'She wasn't alone . . . she was with the man from the fair. . .' Mattie began lamely.

'What man, Mattie? Surely someone would remember him, or her.'

'I told you,' Mattie twisted her hands together in her lap. 'I left the picture with Rosella. She's going to ask.'

'Mattie, she's been with the fair all her life . . . she would have remembered.'

Mattie began shaking her head. She suddenly felt sick and the world seemed to swim about her. She started crying, hot oily tears running down on to the table. 'Shut up, Bram. Please, shut up!'

'What about those three years, Mattie?' He sounded like one of those prosecuting lawyers on TV. 'You've got to admit it, Mary *wanted* to disappear. She told you you were born in the north. Come off it, Mattie. *Every* kid knows where it's born. Why did she never tell you the name of the town? And why was she so paranoid . . . never letting you go anywhere by yourself? And why are there no photographs of you as a baby, no mementos? Everyone keeps things from when their kids were little—'

'Bram, why are you being so horrible?' She almost screamed at him.

He didn't try to deny it. He just stared at her. She looked him in the eye now. His face was flushed. This was hurting him as much as it was hurting her. He was breathing heavily, his intense eyes boring into hers.

He turned the bit of paper towards her and shook it. 'Read it, Mattie. See the date the kid was stolen . . .'

It was there, before her swimming eyes. The date burned her sight.

19th August 1978.

There was a photo too. A photo of a chubby, laughing, dark-haired child waving a toy car in the air. The picture had been photocopied and was not very clear.

Mattie opened her mouth to speak but nothing came out.

Bram thrust the piece of paper back into his pocket. He flicked back his shaggy fringe, not long enough to tie back but too long to stay out of his eyes. 'Mattie,' he said hoarsely. His mouth trembled. 'We've got to find out.'

Mattie nodded wordlessly. He was right, of course.

Bram got up and came round to her side of the booth. He sat down and put his arm round her neck, pulling her close. 'I'm sorry, Mattie. I'm really sorry.' He pulled her head down on his shoulder. Then he took a paper napkin from the glass on the table and wiped her face gently. 'I didn't mean to hurt you.' She could tell by his voice he was almost crying too. 'I just didn't think you'd listen to me unless I made you.'

She took the napkin from him and blew her nose.

'How are we going to find out?' She slid away from him. She couldn't think straight with his arm round her like that. A couple in the next booth were eyeing them curiously.

'Dad said we should go to the police.'

'They'll think we're crazy. . .'

Bram took her hand. She realized he was as scared as she was. 'So be it, Mattie. But we've got to try. Dad reckoned they'll still have all the files.'

Mattie closed her eyes. 'They never found her, then?'

'The doctor wasn't sure. She didn't think so and neither Mum or Dad could remember reading anything about it. You know what it's like. You feel terrible when something like that happens then the next week you've forgotten about it.'

'Bram, the poor kid's probably dead.' Her stomach churned when she thought of all the appalling things that might have happened to the child. The child who was nothing to do with her.

'Maybe, Mattie. Maybe not.'

Suddenly she felt a terrible need. A need to know everything. Where exactly the child had been taken from, what her parents were like, their names . . . everything. She wiped her moist palms on the thighs of her jeans.

'Mattie, it'll be all right.' Bram was looking at her with a face full of compassion.

But it wouldn't be all right. Nothing would ever be the same again.

She realized the waitress had come back and Bram was asking Mattie if she wanted anything to eat. She shook her head and smiled feebly. She leaned her elbows on the table and steepled her hands against her nose. She took a deep breath.

'No thanks.' She thought she'd never eat again.

She looked up. She could see the girl thought Bram was attractive. Her eyes washed over his face as she turned away. Mattie watched as he eyed the girl's legs as she walked down the aisle between the booths. She suddenly wanted his arms around her more than anything. If there was one single thing in her life she could be sure of, it was that. 'Bram?'

He gazed at her.

She fiddled with a stud on her jacket. 'Let's go back.'

She saw his eyes glow as if he was seeing her for the very first time in his life. He smiled and her pulse quickened.

'It's only a single room,' Bram joked as he climbed the stairs behind her. 'There's not room for two, you know.'

Make it all right, Bram, she thought as the enormity of what he'd told her crashed in on her. Please make it all right.

'I'll never let anyone hurt you, Mattie,' he whispered later as they lay like squashed tomatoes on the narrow bed.

'I know and I'm sorry I was such a pig.'

He stroked her hair. 'You weren't . . . you were you.'

'Yes,' Mattie said miserably. 'But who am I?'

'We can't both go down to breakfast,' Mattie said in the morning. 'The old bat will have a fit.' She peered at herself in the mirror. She looked pale, hair spiked up all over the place. She raked it flat with her fingers. She tried desperately to see some resemblance between her and the photocopied image of the child on Bram's bit of paper. She didn't know if she hoped there would be, or if she hoped there wouldn't be.

Bram was sitting up in bed, propped up on one elbow, watching her. 'Mattie, what are we going to do?'

She fiddled with her fingernail. 'You said it was in all the papers.'

'Yes.'

She turned to face him. 'Bram, let's find out as much as we can before we go to the police. I really don't just want to barge in . . .'

'OK,' he said. 'Got any ideas?'

'The newspaper office.' Mattie had lain awake almost all night thinking about it. 'They keep back copies. When I was doing my media studies I went to our local paper to look in the archives. They keep them for years. Right back until the paper was started usually.'

'Porthland's a pretty small place,' Bram said as if she didn't already know. 'Are they likely to have their own paper?'

'I'm not sure, but I saw a copy of the *West Country Herald* on the table downstairs and it was advertising the carnival so it must cover this area.'

'It would have been in all the nationals,' Bram said.

'Yes, but let's try here first, huh?'

'OK, captain.' He flung back the covers and came to stand behind her. She looked at their two reflections. Bram didn't look as if he'd slept much either. He put his hands on her shoulders, running his thumbs over her collarbones. 'Mattie, have you thought—'

'Yes,' she said quickly. 'I've thought about everything.'

The offices of the *West Country Herald* were in the next town. They were just opening up when Mattie and Bram arrived.

'No problem,' one of the journalists said. She had been roped in to man the reception desk as the girl was stuck in a traffic jam. 'We still get lots of requests to see those.'

'Oh?' Mattie's eyebrows shot up.

'Yes.' The woman led them down a long corridor, then up two flights of stairs. 'There's always someone or other writing or researching into missing people.'

Mattie's stomach turned over. She felt her old familiar

urge to run before it was too late. But Bram was holding her hand so tightly she couldn't escape even if she wanted to.

'Did they ever find the kid?' Bram asked.

The woman unlocked a door and held it open for them to go in. 'After you. Did they ever find her? No, not a hope. Disappeared into thin air. The town was packed, you see. Families with kids . . . no one would ever have suspected someone pushing a buggy. The police reckoned the kidnapper nipped on a train and went off into the wide blue yonder. There were loads of witnesses but none of their testimonies ever came to anything.'

'What . . .' Mattie swallowed. 'What do they think happened to her?'

The woman opened a tall, metal cupboard. The door swung back, out of control, and hit the wall with a clang.

The woman sucked at her teeth. 'Dead probably,' she said. 'The world's full of maniacs. Right,' she continued, 'the files are there all in date order. You want 18th August to about 25th. The story had been done to death by then.' She laughed. 'That was a Freudian slip. OK, I'll leave you to it. Just make sure you put them back in the right order, please. Some of you students play hell with our filing system.'

Mattie smiled although she didn't feel a bit like it. 'OK, thanks.'

They stood looking at the mass of bound copies of the *West Country Herald*. Mattie took off her bag and dumped it on the table in the corner of the room. There was no use putting it off any longer.

'Here . . .' Bram had taken out a bunch of files. 'You look at these and I'll take the next lot.'

Mattie's hand shook as she took them from him. She went to the table and placed the files in front of her. This could be it, she thought. This could be the moment I find out who I really am. Or it could be the time I find out who I'm not. She didn't know which one she preferred.

Mattie . . . the thin arm outstretched. The voice, hoarse with pain. *Mattie, I've got something to tell you* . . .

20th August 1978, someone had written in thick, black marker pen on the front of the file.

The banner headline jumped out at her. 'CARNIVAL CHILD KIDNAPPED' and underneath 'Parents' agony as they tell of picnic snooze that ended in heartache'. Underneath was the same photograph of the child that Bram had shown her. Only it was clearer this time. Mattie stared at it. She touched the child's smiling face with her fingertip as if she wanted to feel the texture of its flesh. The dark, almost black hair, the deep brown eyes. It could be anyone . . . anyone . . . anyone . . .

Her heart hammered a wild and crazy beat. Her eyes scanned the report. At the bottom it said, 'turn to page 2 for full story and pictures.'

Mattie slowly turned the page.

In Bram's paper, dated 23rd August, the story had already been relegated to the inside page. 'No Leads on Kidnapped Carnival Kid,' it said. The story went on to report how the police had talked to hundreds of holidaymakers and residents but had no leads on the kidnapped child. A man from Saracen's Fun-fair had spent a brief time in custody as someone reported seeing him lurking in the park at the time the child was taken. But it turned out he was looking for a watch he had lost the day before. There were no other clues. The child had disappeared into thin air and police were already expressing a real fear that she was dead.

Mattie stared at page two. She didn't read the full details. She didn't have to. Without taking her eyes away, she reached blindly for her bag. She opened it, her fingers searching in the front pocket. She pulled out the folded pieces of drawing paper. She didn't know why she had brought the portraits of her people with her to Porthland. She hadn't seen them lately and had begun to think she really would never see them again. She unfolded the paper and laid it on the open newspaper. Her hand was shaking so much she could hardly smooth out the creases . . .

Bram stopped reading when he heard the sound from the far corner of the room. He swivelled round on his seat. Mattie had pulled something out of her bag. It was a picture. Something she had sketched herself. Two people. A man and a woman, misty as if she had been looking at them through a pool of water. She had laid it on the open newspaper. Her head was bowed and she was crying, very quietly, to herself.

Bram sprang from his chair and was beside her in a flash. 'Mattie!'

And then he saw. A newspaper photograph of two people. The headline above. 'Carnival baby's parents beg for her return.'

And next to it, held flat by Mattie's shaking hand, was the picture she had drawn of her people, the people that Mattie could see but no one else could. The people who were always smiling. Only in the *other* picture of them, the one in the newspaper, they weren't smiling at all. In *this* picture their faces were full of anguish as they stared out at Mattie from the pages of the *West Country Herald*.

10

Mattie and Bram sat in the police station waiting room. Mattie stared round at the posters on the wall. Lock your car . . . lock your windows . . . reward offered . . . tell a neighbour you're going away . . . dogs worrying sheep will be shot . . . There was a drinks machine in the corner.

The police sergeant had eyed them suspiciously when they came in. Were people who wore leather jackets and young men with pony-tails potential criminals? They'd asked to see someone about the Sarah Cole kidnapping.

'Doing research, are you?' the sergeant had asked.

Mattie swallowed quickly. 'Something like that,' she said.

'You'd best go to the *Herald*,' suggested the police officer. 'They keep back numbers . . .'

'We've been there.' Bram leaned on the counter. 'We'd like to talk to someone who was on the case, if possible.'

'Please,' said Mattie and there must have been something in her face that made the sergeant suddenly realize how vital it was.

'Take a seat,' she said. 'I'll find out if someone will see you.'

Mattie sat fiddling with the strap on her bag. Bram had gone to the window to look out at the traffic. If they don't hurry up I'll scream, she thought.

Bram came back. 'Fancy something out of the machine?'

Mattie shook her head. 'No thanks.'

Bram sat down. He leaned forward, his elbows on his knees, and tapped his toes to the rhythm of some silent rock music in his head.

A door opened and a man in brown slacks and an open-necked white shirt came through.

'Mattie Browne?' He looked at Bram.

'That's me,' Mattie said.

'Oh.' He eyed Mattie and something like shock passed across his face. He knows, Mattie thought. My God, he knows. He knows I'm Sarah, not Mattie . . . not Mary's daughter but Beverley and Robert's. She still couldn't really take it in. How are you supposed to feel when you find out your whole life's a lie? That you're not the person you thought you were. That you're not the age you thought you were. That your mother wasn't your mother at all but a kidnapper who wrenched a child away from its parents and disappeared into the wide blue yonder?

She introduced Bram and they all shook hands formally.

'I'm Bill Palmer, Inspector.' He didn't take his eyes off her. 'You wanted to talk about the Sarah Cole case?'

'Yes,' said Mattie.

'I was on the case when it happened.' He held the door open and they went through into another office. He dragged two chairs over and invited them to sit down. 'It's a long time ago now but I remember it as if it was yesterday.'

'Yes,' Mattie said.

The inspector still stared at her, narrowing his eyes as if to shut out everything but the sight of her face.

The memory of that moment at the newspaper office crashed into her thoughts. She had sat gazing at the pictures of her people. The portraits she had drawn from memory and the photographs in the newspaper. The same people yet so different. In one, smiling, like parents smile at their kids and say peek-a-boo. The other, two distraught, desperate faces, the woman, even in her agony so like Mattie, begging, begging whoever had taken their daughter to please, please bring her back.

'Do you think that's what Mum wanted to tell me?' she had said when she could eventually speak.

Bram had shaken his head. He was still in a daze, stunned by what he saw.

'What? You mean some kind of deathbed confession?'

Mattie had supposed that was what she meant.

'I don't know,' Bram had gone on. 'Nobody knows.' He had tried to comfort her. 'She must have been desperately lonely and unhappy, Mattie, and you know she had . . . problems.'

'I know . . . but to do that to someone . . .' Mattie had always been scared she had inherited Mary's instability. Now, strangely, it was as if a burden had lifted from her shoulders. She didn't allow herself to think what her real parents were like. They could be a bit . . . well, odd, too. Odder even . . . driven crazy by the loss of their child.

'Why didn't you show me these pictures before, Mattie?' Bram had said. She could tell he was hurt that she had kept them a secret.

'I don't know.'

He had studied them intently, then looked at her. 'I can see the likeness, Mattie. Couldn't you?'

She had shaken her head, wondering how she could have been so blind. 'No . . . it never crossed my mind.'

They had both sat in silence after that. Mattie and Bram. Best friends. Childhood sweethearts. There had been no words either of them could say to describe how they felt. Just the contact, the hand held tightly. It seemed to be enough.

'Right.' The inspector took his seat on the other side of the desk. His hand shook slightly as he fiddled with his pen.

Mattie came to. He's pretending, she thought. He's pretending he doesn't know. He's got his official police mask on but underneath he's as stunned as we are.

'What can I do for you, then?'

But she didn't know where to start. Her heart thudded and her palms were sweating. She leaned forward, hugging her arms round herself. Bram was looking at her, willing her to say something. She glanced desperately at him. He grinned at her and nodded.

'Fire away,' he said.

So she swallowed and began her story.

Half-way through, the inspector picked up the phone and asked for mugs of coffee to be sent in. A young officer brought them on a tray. He glanced curiously at Mattie's white face and red-rimmed eyes then went out without saying a word.

Bram sat in silence, his face grim, while she finished.

Bill Palmer hadn't said a word either. He had just leaned back in his chair, listening intently. His expression gave nothing away. Once or twice, when Mattie faltered, he had frowned. He had handed her a tissue from the box on his desk when she cried. He had waited patiently for her to recover and continue with her tale.

When she'd finished, he picked up the phone.

'Bring in the Sarah Cole file will you, Sue.' He sounded calm, looked calm, yet Mattie knew his mind was a whirlpool, just like hers.

The file was so thick the sergeant could hardly carry it. Bram rose to help as she moved papers aside to dump it on the desk.

'Thanks.' She smiled at him as if she had changed her mind about leather jackets.

Without saying a word, the inspector thumbed thoughtfully through the mountain of papers. Every now and then he glanced at Mattie. Then he began his questions.

'You say there's no record of where you and your mum were between 1978 and 1981.'

Mattie sniffed and shook her head. 'No . . . no medical records anyway.'

'And you don't remember where you lived?'

I've told you, she thought. Please don't make me go over it again.

Bram ran his hand over his hair. 'She's told you all that,' he piped up.

'I know but I need to make sure.'

'It's OK.' Mattie glanced at Bram. Strangely, she felt bet-

131

ter . . . as if telling the whole story had somehow cleared her mind. It was up to the police now. By coming here . . . by visiting Saracen's, by letting the hypnotherapist invade her subconscious, she had done all she could. 'No,' she answered firmly. 'I don't remember anything. I know we lived in Yorkshire later and I remember a row of terraced houses with walled-in back yards but nothing else.'

'And these *people*? You say Amery told you they were definitely someone from your past.'

'He said they *could* be. Look . . .' Mattie leaned forward. She *had* to make him believe her. 'I know I could easily have copied their likenesses from newspaper archives. But I didn't, honestly. Until Doctor Kirkpatrick remembered why she'd heard of Porthland I'd got no idea who they might be or that they had any connection with the place at all. Mr Amery said they were just *someone* I could have come across as a kid. People who, for some reason or other, had stuck in my memory.'

Inspector Palmer took a pen from his desk and chewed the end thoughtfully. 'You see the thing is, Mattie, I could very easily contact Mr and Mrs Cole and tell them what you've told me. In fact, they still come to see me every year in the hope that there's some news of Sarah. But the trouble is . . . they're still so desperate that I think they'd be ready to believe anyone who walked in here and claimed to be her. Especially someone like you, Mattie. Dark hair, eyes . . . roughly the right age Sarah would have been if— We need to have proof, Mattie . . . proof.'

She felt a flush coming to her cheeks. 'I'm not *claiming* to be anyone,' she said angrily. 'I . . . we . . . just thought we should come and tell you what's happened.'

'What would be the point of making it up?' said Bram sharply. 'They're not millionaires or anything are they?'

Bill Palmer shook his head. 'No.' He rose and began pacing around the room. He sat back down in his chair, leaned his elbow on his hand and chewed his fingernail. 'Mattie, can you think of anything . . . anything that might

132

prove you're Sarah Cole? You know she would have been eighteen by now?'

'I know,' Mattie said. She felt like telling him she could add up, just like anyone else but there wouldn't have been any point. She had always been bright and mature for her age. She had even started her periods before most people in her class. But seventeen, eighteen . . . She felt shattered. Was it really true? She was a whole year older than she'd thought? It was the craziest thing she'd ever heard.

They were both looking at her, waiting for an answer.

'I'm sorry, I can't think of anything.'

She'd nearly had enough. She was ready to go home, forget all about it. Be the birthdayless, motherless Mattie Browne for the rest of her life. Who cared?

'If I did I'd have told you, wouldn't I?' She half rose from the chair. Bram looked at her, startled. 'OK,' she said angrily. 'Let's forget the whole thing, shall we?'

'No!' Bill Palmer's voice was too loud and too anxious.

'I don't want to upset anyone,' Mattie said.

'You're not. Please sit down, Mattie.'

'You could talk to Doctor Kirkpatrick,' Bram said. 'And that hypnotist bloke.'

'Yes, I intend to.'

Mattie sat back down and searched in her bag for her note book. 'I can give you her number.'

'Yes, thanks.'

'And Mr Amery's. He gave me his card.'

Bill Palmer waved his hand. 'It's all right, I know Charles.'

He sat looking thoughtful for a moment or two then turned to the back of the file. He drew out an envelope. Then he stared at Mattie in the same way he'd stared at her when they first met. 'I had this done a few months ago.' He took something out. 'The case has bugged me for years and years. They're such good people, the Coles. They've never forgiven themselves for what happened. All they did was put the poor kid in the shade under the trees and accidentally doze off for ten minutes. I remember Beverley telling me how Sarah loved watching the movement of leaves in the breeze . . .'

'Yes,' said Mattie.

'Mattie . . .' He gazed at her and she saw a bright spark of hope flare in his eyes. 'Don't get me wrong, we'll still need proof, but this, and your uncanny resemblance to Beverley Cole, is good enough for me.'

She wondered what he was holding in his hand. Another photograph? They had already looked at loads of Sarah as a baby. In the pram. In the garden. With her gran. On the beach in Porthland taken the day before she disappeared. Mattie had recognized the place immediately. It had been where she had seen her people, sitting by the rocks. She had felt awkward telling the inspector, but still he had listened in silence. He had simply handed her the pictures without comment then studied her face as she looked at them.

And then he showed her what he had taken from the file.

'It's the latest thing,' he explained. 'The computer guys study old photographs and create an image of what they think the child would look like . . . in this case, Mattie, seventeen years on. It's easier with girls, their faces don't alter so much at puberty as boys.'

Mattie stared at the computer-generated image. Her heart thudded.

Beside her, Bram drew in his breath.

'It's you, Mattie.' His voice seemed to be coming from another planet.

'Yes,' she whispered. She wondered how many more shocks she could take. 'It's me.' She stared up at the inspector. 'You knew, didn't you?'

He passed his hand over his face. 'Mattie, I've always hoped this would happen. When I first saw you I knew you *could* be Sarah. But this . . .' He pointed to the computer image. '. . . seems to me to prove it. But again, we've got to have evidence, Mattie.' He cleared his throat noisily. 'You know us coppers are a soft old lot, really.'

'Yeah?' said Bram and, strangely, they all burst out laughing.

And later in the station canteen, Bill Palmer said, 'What about that proof, Mattie?'

Mattie shook her head and gazed at him mournfully. 'I can't think of anything. Mum must have covered our tracks so carefully.'

'Well, we'll make enquiries, of course. We'll start here in Porthland. You said your mum told her parents she was going off with a bloke from the fair?'

Mattie nodded. 'Yes . . . but I see now that she probably didn't. She must have planned it all down to the last detail. She *knew* her mum and dad wouldn't tell anyone she'd gone off with someone like that . . . so no one thought it weird when they said she'd gone to live with an aunt in London.'

The inspector chewed his lip. 'You know we made enquiries at all the ports . . . abroad . . . Ireland . . . everywhere,' he sighed and shook his head. 'Blanks . . . all blanks. I don't see what good it would do to go over all that again.' He leaned forward across the table. 'No, Mattie . . . I'm beginning to think the proof's got to come from you.'

Mattie looked at Bram hopelessly. She racked her brains. There had to be something . . .

11

Mattie sat bolt upright. She had suddenly remembered something. Something important. It had come to her in her sleep.

An arrow of moonlight pierced the gap between the curtains, violating the sad darkness of the room. They quivered in the warm wind that blew softly in from the sea. Moonlight danced on the bed and suddenly they were there . . . the man, the woman. They came towards Mattie, silver grey in the moon-sliced darkness, smiling . . . hands moving over faces. The woman, Beverley, loomed close . . . 'Peek-a-boo.' So they hadn't disappeared for ever after all.

Mattie shook Bram's shoulder fiercely.

'What . . .?' He sat up in a daze of sleep. 'Mattie . . . are you OK?'

'Bram . . . get up, we've got to go home.'

'Don't be daft, it's the middle of the night.'

'Bram, I've remembered something.'

Bram rubbed his eyes. 'What?'

'The bracelet.' Her heart thudded wildly. It was the expanding type. It could have fitted a tiny baby or a toddler. Why hadn't she looked at it more closely?

'What bracelet, Mattie?'

She told him, quickly. Words tumbling out, sentences not making sense.

'Hold on, hold on . . .?' He pushed back his hair. 'What makes you think it wasn't one Mary bought you?'

'Because when I think about it it was really tiny. OK, it stretched much bigger but it was definitely a baby's bracelet.'

'Mattie, none of the reports in the paper mentioned a bracelet.'

'I know.' She felt like a drowning man, clutching any piece of flotsam that floated her way. 'But it's the only thing I can think of that might be connected with . . .' She could hardly say the name. ' . . . Sarah.'

Bram suddenly grinned. 'I'm kidding you, Mattie . . . if you say it was a baby's bracelet then I, for one, am prepared to believe you.'

Mattie's heart was suddenly full of wild hope. She planted a fierce kiss on his forehead. 'Thanks, Bram.'

He yawned. 'But it's waited seventeen years, can't it wait until morning?'

Mattie lay down with a sigh. 'OK, I suppose it can.' She pulled the sheet up around her chin. 'You know,' she said softly, 'my people . . . they used to say a name but it was never mine.'

Bram turned and put his mouth against her shoulder. 'Was it Sarah?'

'I could never make out what it was . . . but I suppose it must have been.' She suddenly felt terror and apprehension invade her mind. 'Bram . . . it's really scary.'

'I know. But it'll be OK, Mattie. Honestly it will.'

'We'll miss the carnival,' Mattie said as they drove past the fairground, 'and Madame Rosella's still got Mum's photograph.'

Bram glanced at her swiftly. 'Do you want to go and get it, then?'

Mattie shook her head. 'No,' she said sorrowfully. 'I don't think I want it back, to be honest.'

Bram touched her hand. 'Mattie, whatever Mary did . . . she loved you very much.'

'I know.' Mattie hunched her shoulders against the pain. 'That's the trouble.'

They had phoned Bill Palmer and told him they were going back.

'He sounded weird on the phone,' Mattie said. 'As if

there was something he wanted to tell me but couldn't get it out.'

Bram frowned. 'What exactly did he say then?'

'Well . . . nothing . . . really, it was just his tone of voice.'

'You know you *are* psychic, Mattie. You can always tell things about people.'

Mattie shrugged. He was right . . . but she had always thought she was just perceptive, gauging people's moods from their faces, their eyes. Sometimes knowing what they were going to say before they said it. Was that psychic? Mum . . . Mary . . . had always said she had an artistic temperament. She remembered what Bram had said when she told him.

'You said I was just moody,' she laughed.

He looked indignant. 'Who, me? When?'

'When Mum said I had an artistic temperament.'

'Same thing,' he grinned.

She made a fist and thumped him on the leg. 'What will you call me?' she said, suddenly sober.

'A twit,' he said.

'No . . . seriously. If I'm definitely her . . . will you call me Sarah?'

'No.' His voice sounded strange and when she glanced at him his face was sad. 'No, you'll always be Mattie to me.'

'Bram, I feel excited and scared and . . . God I don't know *what* I feel.' She leaned back in the seat and ran her hands through her hair. 'Bram, this really blows my mind.'

'That's nothing to what it's going to do to *their* minds when they find out you're alive.'

A thought struck her. 'Bram, I think they *know* I'm alive . . . remember what Rosella said . . . if you're seeing them, maybe they're seeing you too.'

'Yes. Well, with a bit of luck you'll soon find out.'

'Yes.'

But it wasn't luck they needed, it was proof.

Mattie shivered as if a sudden shadow had passed over Mary's grave.

As they crested the hill, Mattie suddenly wanted to take one last look at Porthland for the time being. She knew she would return one day. To the house in Lilac Avenue, to the fair . . . maybe one day even to the Carnival. But for now she just wanted to look over the cliff top, just to make sure she hadn't dreamed the whole thing.

'Can you stop a minute, Bram?'

'Sure . . .'

The Mini pulled up in the lay-by overlooking the town. Mattie got out and stood gazing at the view. A shaft of sunlight hit the horizon and turned it silver. The tide-washed beach below was deserted apart from a couple taking an early morning walk along the sparkling shore. Mattie could see their pale blue Volvo parked by the slipway. The woman was barefoot, carrying her shoes in one hand. Their dark heads were bowed and Mattie could tell by the set of their shoulders that they were sad about something. Maybe they'd had a row? She took in a deep breath of sea air. It was hard to be unhappy on such a beautiful morning.

Mattie dragged her eyes away from them and gazed out to sea. She let herself be mesmerized by the gentle rise and fall of the waves. She felt full of sorrow, yet full of happiness at the same time. A crazy mixture of emotions. She closed her eyes but she could still see the picture imprinted on her mind. The shining sea, the sand . . . the couple walking along the beach. Things change, she said to herself, we move on, our lives turn one way, then the other. She had thought herself lost, as if she had strayed into another country where black was white and day, night and someone had turned the signposts round and she had become completely disorientated. But now, Mattie had the sudden, overwhelming feeling that the path was opening up in front of her and she would find her way home at last.

She opened her eyes. Bram was beside her, watching a trawler chug its way towards the gleaming horizon. She sought his hand and he squeezed it absent mindedly.

'Come on,' she said. 'Let's get going.'

* * *

'Did you have any luck?' They had called in at the shop to tell Katherine they were home.

They exchanged glances. Then Mattie quickly told her what had happened.

When she had finished, Katherine looked stunned. 'I still can't believe Mary would have done a thing like that,' she said. 'When Doctor Kirkpatrick phoned me I remembered the stories in all the papers. But for it to be someone you knew, a friend . . .' Her voice broke and she shook her head ruefully. 'You know, I've been dreading you turning up on the doorstep and telling me just this.'

'But it all seems to fit, Katherine. And Inspector Palmer thinks I'm Sarah. He just needs some kind of proof.'

'But what? I mean, if this is all true, Mary would have been silly to keep anything of Sarah's, wouldn't she?'

Then Mattie told her about the bracelet.

'You'd better go and find it then,' Katherine said. 'If those poor people are your real parents, Mattie, then I reckon they've waited long enough, don't you?'

'Yes,' Mattie said.

She suddenly felt as if she was on a roller coaster and the sooner she got to solid ground, the better.

'Here it is.' Mattie held up the envelope with its soft tissue-wrapped parcel inside. She drew out the bracelet.

Bram took it from her fingers. 'Wow, you're right.' He squeezed it so it made a tiny circle. 'It *is* a baby's one. It's almost as small as that identity band of mine Mum's got.'

Mattie wrapped it back up carefully. 'I'll go and phone Bill Palmer.'

The inspector picked up the phone immediately as if he had been waiting for her call.

'Describe it to me, Mattie,' he said.

'It's just a plain silver bracelet.'

'How big?'

'About three centimetres across but it expands to about six or seven centimetres.'

'OK, Mattie. Now, I'll tell you what I'm going to do. I'm going to phone the Coles and ask them if Sarah was wearing any jewellery.'

'I can't understand why it wasn't mentioned in the description of her,' Mattie said. She had been puzzling over it ever since she remembered coming across it in Mum's bureau.

'No, neither can I. The only thing I can say is that in all the panic, it may well have been overlooked. You'd be surprised how descriptions can differ. I remember Robert had sworn Sarah was wearing a white T-shirt whereas Beverley insisted it was yellow.'

'OK,' Mattie said. 'You'll let me know what they say?'

'Of course.'

Mattie put the phone down with a sigh. 'All we've got to do now,' she said, feeling as if she could burst. 'Is wait.'

Kelly

Kelly was watching TV when the phone rang. It was showjumping and she couldn't bear to miss it so she yelled out to her gran.

'Phone's ringing, Gran.'

Her grandmother was in the garden, finishing off a painting she was doing of the startling blue delphiniums that grew along one side of the wall. She put down her brush and rose from her stool.

'Coming.'

Inspector Palmer was just about to give up when Robert's mother answered. There had been no reply from the Coles' house but he had a list of numbers on file to call if there was any news. He often marvelled at the Coles'capacity to cling on to their hopes for Sarah. When they hadn't yet called in on him this August, he had begun to wonder if, at last, that hope was fading.

'Mrs Cole, it's Bill Palmer.'

He could tell by the old lady's voice that her heart turned over at the sound of his voice.

'Inspector Palmer!' she said. 'How nice to hear you.'

In the sitting room, Kelly overheard the name. She'd never met Bill Palmer but she'd heard her parents speak of him so often he seemed like an old friend. What on earth could he want? Dad had told her once that in the early years, every time they heard the phone they thought it might be someone ringing to tell them they had found Sarah, or her dead body. Kelly used to have nightmares about it. Seeing in her dreams her sister's tiny corpse lying in the ground somewhere being eaten by worms.

Kelly forgot all about the showjumping and turned down the TV so she could hear what Gran was saying.

'I'm sorry, they're away.' Gran's voice was full of apprehension. 'In fact they've gone to Porthland as usual. Haven't they contacted you?'

Kelly heard her gran move the chair and sit down as if she was getting ready for a long conversation.

'Well, I'm sure they intend to, Bill. They were stopping off on the way down and didn't think they'd arrive until late last night depending on the traffic. They'll probably get in touch with you later today. Has . . .' Gran hesitated. 'Has something happened?'

Kelly heard a small exclamation of surprise. 'Oh, I see.'

Gran listened for a moment or two longer. 'All right, Bill. If they don't come and see you I'll tell them you called. They're bound to phone to tell us they've arrived safely. No, I'm sorry. I don't know where they're staying. They hadn't booked anywhere. All right. Goodbye.'

By now, Kelly was standing in the doorway. Somehow the importance of the showjumping had paled into insignificance. She saw Gran sit for a moment with her head in her hands. Then she seemed to pull herself together. She looked up to see Kelly.

'That was Inspector Palmer,' she said.

'I heard. What did he want?'

'To see your mum and dad.' Gran was being cagey, she could tell.

'What for?'

'He didn't really say. Just that something might have come up.'

Kelly could see the bright spark of hope in Gran's eyes. How can she do it, she thought. After all this time . . . how can she still hope Sarah's alive?

She went and put her hand on her grandmother's shoulder. 'What do you think it might be, Gran?'

Mrs Cole rubbed her eyes. She stood up and gave Kelly a hug. 'I don't know, darling. There's been nothing for so long.' She pushed back a stray lock of her granddaughter's hair. 'It's not that I've given up . . . none of us have. It's just

. . .' She shook her head. 'Sometimes I think if she's dead, I'd rather not know.'

'I don't think Mum and Dad feel like that.'

'No, Kelly. They're very brave people, your mum and dad. I would have gone mad long ago.'

Kelly could see she was near to tears. Her heart turned over. Poor Gran . . . poor Mum and Dad . . . poor Sarah, poor everybody.

Kelly arrived back from a morning ride with her friend to Gran's apprehensive face.

'Your mum and dad phoned,' she said. 'They're going to see the inspector straight away.'

Kelly waited in for the rest of the day but there was no news. Gran was going around in a dream. She had packed away her painting stuff saying she couldn't concentrate, then sat in a chair staring out of the window and twisting her hands together in her lap.

Kelly hung around, watched TV, sat in the garden with her Walkman, read a bit—still no one rang back.

In the end, neither she nor her grandmother could stand it any longer. 'I'm going to ring Bill Palmer,' Gran said, thumbing through her telephone book.

Kelly saw her gran tapping her fingers impatiently on the table while she waited for the police station to answer. Then, when they did, it was only to tell her that Inspector Palmer had left and wouldn't be back for a day or two.

Mrs Cole slammed down the phone. 'They wouldn't give me any information.' She ran her hand agitatedly through her hair. It already stood up like a brush around her head. Kelly almost giggled although she didn't know why. She thought she must be getting hysterical.

She went to link her arm through her gran's. She'd had enough of hanging around. 'Come on, Gran, let's go for a walk. They're bound to let us know if there's any news.'

* * *

Later that evening a car drew up at the door. Gran had been dozing in the chair while Kelly watched *EastEnders*. The actors were flashing before her eyes, walking . . . talking . . . arguing, but Kelly didn't have a clue what they were on about. All she could think about was Mum and Dad and what the inspector might have told them.

When she heard the car she jumped up. 'Gran . . . someone's here.'

She went to look out of the window. It was just beginning to get dark outside but she could easily make out her dad's car parked by the kerb. She turned. 'It's Mum and Dad. What on earth are they doing back so soon?'

Gran's face went pale. Her eyes widened behind her glasses. Kelly went and clasped her hands between her own. Her gran was shaking. 'Come on, Gran. It'll be OK,' she said, although she didn't know who she was trying to convince.

Three people were getting out of the car. Mum and Dad and a tall stranger. They walked up the path. Dad in front, Mum behind, the stranger holding her arm.

'. . . and you'd forgotten all about the bracelet,' Kelly said later when she had heard the full story.

Her mum shook her head. 'We hadn't exactly forgotten about it. It's just that *I* thought Dad had taken it off, and he thought I had. We'd planned to take Sarah in the sea if it was warm enough and thought the salt water might spoil the silver.'

'And then you packed your stuff up to come home,' Kelly went on, 'and didn't find out until months later that the box was empty.' She could just imagine her mum going through Sarah's things. Crying, hugging Sarah's favourite toys to her face. Mum had told her it was months before she could even go into Sarah's room, let alone sort out her toys and clothes.

'That's right,' Beverley said. She looked pale and drawn, as if she hadn't slept for days. 'I was unpacking the holiday bag months later when I realized the box was empty. It seemed too late to tell anyone then.'

Kelly stared at the inspector. He was just as she had imagined him. Burly, with iron-grey hair and dark eyebrows. What had surprised her was that he was wearing jeans and a T-shirt. She'd imagined that it was only the whizz-kid undercover agents that wore that kind of stuff. When they were introduced he had shaken her hand and said she was the image of her mother.

'Poor thing,' Mum said and they had all laughed.

And now, later, sitting in the front room, Kelly had heard all about the bracelet and the dark-haired, pale-faced girl who had come to Bill Palmer and said she thought she might be Sarah. Mum and Dad had listened intently, even though they had heard it all before. They had held hands and now and then had looked at each other and smiled.

Kelly suddenly felt full of dread. If this girl wasn't Sarah she thought they'd go barmy. But if she was . . . she couldn't begin to think what it would be like, having a sister . . . a sister whose shadow had been there for all of her life, yet who she never, ever seriously thought she would meet. The thought was weird and scary and exciting all at once.

Gran and Mum had gone out to make coffee. Dad sat on the sofa, his elbows on his knees, staring at the floor.

'What happens now?' Kelly had almost not dared to ask.

'Someone's gone to fetch them,' the inspector told her.

'Them?'

'She came with her boyfriend. I think she'd like him with her. They seemed very close.'

Kelly pushed her glasses up on her nose. 'What's she like?' she asked him timidly.

'She's like you,' he said. 'Tall, very dark . . . very sensitive. She's had a strange life, Kelly. Her . . . the woman who took her away was very neurotic. I don't think it's been easy for Mattie.'

'Sarah, you mean,' Kelly said quickly. She already felt some strange obligation to defend this sister of hers . . . this

147

ghost who had been part of her life for as long as she could remember.

The inspector pulled a face. 'I think you're going to have to call her Mattie . . . it's how she thinks of herself.'

'It doesn't matter,' Robert said sharply, too sharply. 'It doesn't matter *what* she's called.'

When Kelly glanced at her father he was twisting his hands together in his lap. He was sweating, too. She could see beads of it like little crystals on his forehead. Dad was right. The girl could be called Ermintrude for all Kelly cared.

'When will they arrive?' Kelly asked the inspector.

'Some time tomorrow . . . when you're back home.'

'Mr Palmer,' Kelly said. 'You *are* sure, aren't you? You are sure it's her?'

'Your sister's name was engraved on the inside of the bracelet,' Bill told her. 'I asked your mum and dad's permission *not* to tell Mattie that until she gets here with it.'

'But it'll be awful if it isn't there,' Kelly argued. 'You'll have got their hopes up for nothing.'

The inspector looked at her. 'Kelly, I'm convinced enough to take that risk. You see, if she is an impostor and I told her about the engraving she could very quickly have had it done.'

'Yes,' Kelly said. 'I suppose she could.'

'This way we'll be absolutely certain.'

Kelly didn't know how she was going to be able to wait until tomorrow. It was going to be the longest night of her life.

Mattie

12

'You have got it with you, haven't you?' Bram said as the police car swung down the slip road and on to the motorway.

Mattie patted her pocket. 'Yes.'

'Been to this part of the world before?' the policewoman driving the car looked at them in her rear view mirror. They sat close, Mattie's shoulder touching Bram's. It gave her a feeling of comfort.

'No.' Mattie stared at the fields flashing past. In the distance, the motorway cut a ribbon through rolling downland.

'I have,' Bram said. 'I come this way quite a bit.' It seemed crazy that he had almost passed the Coles' door on his way to the channel ports with his dad.

'Nice part, I always think,' the policewoman said.

'Yes.'

Mattie didn't feel like chatting. Her mind was stretching far ahead. It was enough to cope with, knowing the most momentous thing in your whole life was just about to happen. And knowing that you weren't only going to meet your real parents for the first time, you'd suddenly got a thirteen-year-old sister too.

It seemed bizarre. Like something out of those fantasy novels Bram was so fond of. There was something about the whole thing that still puzzled her though. The inspector said there was one last link in the chain that had to be joined before they could be sure. It still wasn't enough. Mattie's drawing of her people. Her resemblance to Beverley Cole. The bracelet. There had to be one more thing and however much she'd pleaded he wouldn't tell her what it was.

'Mattie, he must be sure or else he'd never bring you to meet them,' Bram had said.

'I know. But it's scary just the same.'

But, for once, he hadn't managed to convince her. Bill Palmer had something up his sleeve and whatever it was she was so frightened she almost didn't come.

Mattie put her hand into her inside pocket and patted the envelope. It was there, the key to her future. She looked at Bram. He was leaning his head against the back of the seat, his eyes closed. As if he felt her looking, he opened them quickly. He grinned at her. Whatever happens, she thought, I'll always want him with me. I couldn't have done any of this without him.

She drew out the envelope and took the tiny silver bracelet from its wrapping. Bram raised his eyebrows and took it from her hand. He ran his fingers over the metal, warm from her body heat. He held it up. Suddenly Mattie noticed something . . . someone's name engraved on the inside.

'Hey.' Her heart thudded as she took it from his hand.

'What?'

Mattie frowned. She couldn't quite make out what it was. 'There's something written inside.' She held it up to the car window so she could see better.

'It's tiny, I can't read it. Oh . . . yes I can.' She turned to Bram, her eyes gleaming with joy and triumph. 'It says "Sarah".'

A great, crazy, crooked smile split Bram's face in two. The driver must have thought they were nuts . . . hugging and kissing and laughing like that. Mattie caught sight of her, staring at them in the mirror. She didn't care. She knew . . . now . . . everything was going to be all right. Suddenly she wasn't frightened any more. She thought, probably, in the whole of her life, she would never be scared of anything again.

The car drove slowly through the village, went up a hill then turned into a narrow lane. It went past a farm and pulled up outside a black and white timbered cottage. Mattie could see a stable at the back, two horses looking over doors as if they were waiting patiently for something. In the front garden, the leaves of an oak tree danced in the breeze. The sun, shining through, made patterns on the grass verge and up the brick path that led to the front door.

She suddenly felt sick. Beside her, Bram was holding her hand so tightly it hurt. Then, the front door opened and two people came out. A man . . . a woman . . . their faces older, yet so familiar to Mattie it was as if she had seen them yesterday. They hovered on the step as if uncertain what to do. Then, someone pushed through and a girl appeared. She had long, dark, almost black, hair and a tanned skin. She wore glasses. After one heart-stopping moment, Mattie saw her look up and say something to the man and woman . . . then she ran down the path towards the car.

Mattie put her fingers on the handle and thrust open the door.